THE CHARMING WINTER

THE CHARMING WINTER

(Rewind #3)

TRACY KRIMMER

For Lin

I never expected my shift at the grocery store to start like this. Someone has arranged the eggplants and peaches in a lewd display. I'm thankful that Bernice, the sweet elderly produce manager, doesn't understand why this is offensive. Her gray hair is pulled back in a ponytail, a style usually reserved for toddlers, yet she somehow manages to make it look good.

When I ask if she has seen who did this, she shakes her head, and a single strand of hair escapes from her ponytail. "It was like this when I came in."

"What time did you arrive?" I'm not in the mood to play detective, but if an employee did this, I have to deal with them.

"A little after six."

Bernice is a top-notch employee, a retired teacher who joined the store as a part-time employee eight years ago. She's like a grandmotherly figure to many of us, so I doubt she'd rat out any of the employees—even Scottie.

I loathe Scottie Silver, the nineteen-year-old son of the owner. We've never been on friendly terms, but I tolerate him since his mother signs my paychecks. Taking a step back and inspecting the display, I notice a pattern; could it be a word?

"Bernice, do you think this spells something?" I inquire.

"Oh, I don't know, dear." Bernice lowers her glasses and squints. "I think that's an A. I'm no artist, though." She points to three eggplants laid out that way. "And that one, too."

"Badass."

"Excuse me?"

"I'm sorry, Bernice. Pardon my language. The display spells out badass; that's what I'm saying."

She slides her glasses back over the bridge of her nose. "Oh, Lord. You're right. I'll clean this up right away." Without another word, she starts picking up the peaches and eggplant, racing them back to their homes. I don't think I've ever seen anyone run as quickly as her. She has a lot of spring in her step for someone in her seventies—more than I do at thirty-eight.

"Thank you. I'll review the security footage and find out who did this." Even though I'm certain of the culprit.

Bernice is getting a raise this year. Truth.

I head back to the security office, where I find none other than Scottie Silver tipped back in a chair, hands behind his head, smacking his gum so loud that I heard him before I even entered the room.

"Four on the floor." I make a peace sign with both hands and jerk my fingers down like chair legs. The last thing I need is for him to fall backward and crack his head open on the hard floor.

"Last time I checked, you weren't my mom. Though you'd make a pretty hot one."

I can feel my cheeks heat up as I try to stifle my anger. Under normal circumstances, I would never accept such a comment from someone, and I know I should stand up for myself. Yet, this person is the son of the owner. If I fire him, I'd likely lose *my* job. My fists clench as I struggle with how to react.

Nope. I'm staying at my parent's house for the time being. Thanks to my ex-husband's carelessness and gambling addiction, I have no choice but to rely on my meager salary for the foreseeable future.

It's been a rude awakening, moving back into my childhood home after being gone for nearly two decades. Mom expects me for dinner every night, Dad controls the television, and they even put a curfew in place for me! I can almost feel the eyes of my dad's police officer buddy, William Reisenberg, watching me from across the street. No one wants to hang out at my parent's house, so my only social life is my weekly meetup at The Copper Fig with my sister, Vivienne, and our friends, Sadie and Dani.

My last date was over the summer with some doofus I picked up at the store.

My sex life has become as dry and lifeless as the overcooked turkey my mom had served on Thanksgiving.

Even that tough, brittle bird got more attention when someone stuffed it full of herbs and spices.

"I need to see the security footage from last night until this morning around six." Scottie keeps his eye on the current scene of the store, still smacking his gum and working my last nerve.

"No can do, *Miss James*."

I want to slap the gum right out of his mouth. An outsider may not pick up on the sarcasm in Scottie's tone, but I feel it through to my bones. I loved Owen, but I hated my rhyming, married name. Holly LaDolly. Once divorced, I raced to return to using my maiden name, making sure all my coworkers knew to refer to me as such. Scottie likes to test me. Every. Single. Day.

"Scottie, someone tampered with the eggplants and peaches in produce. I need to review the footage to see who's responsible."

"Tampered? Like what?"

"They created a," I clear my throat, "display with them."

"I get it." He forms an O with his thumb and pointer finger and shoves his other pointer finger through it multiple times.

"Stop. Completely inappropriate."

"Hey, I only want to ensure I understand the big deal." He holds his hands in the air to show he is no longer acting like a disgusting pig, though I think that's how he lives his entire life.

"Now, please show it to me."

Scottie points to his name tag. "Do you see what it says under my name? Security. I can review the data if you'd like, or you can submit a request in writing to the store owner, my mother, for access."

I'm ready to stomp my foot on the ground like a toddler. He's doing this because *he's* the one who did it. I'm sure of it. Few people are here nightly for restocking, cleaning, and security.

"Isn't your shift almost over?"

"It is, but I'll let Loren know you'll be making a request."

Damn it. Scottie is going to block me from viewing this today. I'm too busy to argue with him, and Loren won't budge, either. Yes, the protocol is that I request access to view unless there is a suspicion of theft or inappropriate activity *at that moment*, which I can view immediately and then submit a report after the fact.

"Would you look at that?" Scottie points to the screen that displays the produce department. "Bernice, the precious soul she is, has already finished cleaning up the sexual display. No harm, no foul. Agree?"

He cocks his head at me while blowing a bubble, the bright pink popping when it achieves its greatness. I can't stand his beady brown eyes and pimply face, yet this is what I have to put up with almost every day of my life.

"Fine," I say, vowing here and now that I won't spend another full year at this place dealing with Scottie's juvenile crap. I'm better than this.

I slam the door on my way out, ready for this day to be over.

And it's only just started.

2

Eight long, grueling hours later, I stumble through the front door, the exhaustion of the day weighting heavily on me. My mom welcomes me with a hug, then asks if I want supper.

"No, thank you. I'm not that hungry."

"Sweetie, you need to eat. You're skin and bones." She stirs the bowl of mashed potatoes before setting them on the table.

My fingers trace the shape of my body, feeling the dip in my waist where it used to be full. Divorce has been hard on me, and I've lost my appetite from time to time.

"I'll eat something later. Promise."

My mom gives a hesitant nod. "Your mail is on the table."

"Thanks." I scoop the envelopes off the counter and head upstairs to my bedroom.

When I first moved back to my parent's house, I stayed in the basement. It felt like my own space, just for me. But after three days of nonstop rain flooded the basement, I moved to my childhood bedroom.

Now it feels a little weird. My twin bed with gold posts

still rests against the wall, sunflowers filling the duvet. My mom has taken down all of my teenage decorations and replaced them with wicker baskets filled with fake flowers and antique pictures. I keep thinking I'll leave this place sooner than later. Every week that passes by, I hope I'm inching closer, but it only feels like I'm pulling back. I'm saving my money, though, and hopefully I can finally have a place of my own soon.

I look over the envelopes littering my bed. Most of them are annoying junk mail, but one of them has a return address that catches my eye—Levi Walsh. It's been years since I've seen him, since Amy's death. She had been my best friend, and it felt so unfair to have her taken away at such a young age. The Walsh family moved away shortly after, and I had lost touch, not knowing where they were or how to find them. It was a different era, the nineties, without the ability to search for people online.

I assumed they left so they could have a fresh start. I can't blame them.

I'm perplexed why Levi is reaching out now. Even more interesting is the return address is in town.

I run my finger along the seam of the envelope, feeling the thin ribbons of glue that cling stubbornly to the paper. I carefully peel open the flap and withdraw a folded, lined sheet of paper. As I unfold it, a wavering smile tugs at my lips; the letter is handwritten and not typed, something almost forgotten in this age of technology. His handwriting is cramped and tight but still neat enough to read.

Dear Holly,

I hope this letter finds you well. I know it's been a very long time since we spoke. We're adults now! It's hard to believe that we never imagined this age so many years ago, yet here we are.

I sent this to your parent's house, hoping you would

receive it. I haven't kept in touch with anyone, and since my mom passed away two years ago, I don't know if she still spoke with anyone. I assumed if I sent this letter to this address, somehow you'd receive it.

Now that my mom is gone, it's just my dad and me. Dad isn't doing well, and I have moved him into a nursing home. I moved back to town, and I'm renting a place in Holbrook to be near him. When cleaning their house, I found some of Amy's things. There was something I thought you might want, but I didn't want to mail it in case you didn't receive it.

Call me if you'd like to meet up and I can give you the item. I enclosed my phone number, and you have my address from the envelope. I hope to hear from you soon.

Sincerely yours,

Levi Walsh

My vision blurs as I wipe the tears from my eyes. A few drops land on the letter, distorting some words. When was the last time I let Amy cross my mind? I tried so hard to move on from losing her, and now Levi has something of hers for me.

I try to remember what we used to do when we were together. We'd huddle around the kitchen table, playing card games and singing along to songs on the radio. She'd get a buzzing feeling of excitement when a chain letter landed in the mailbox. Though the stories were often silly or downright scary, she loved them. At night, she'd insist on watching a horror movie and I'd hide under the blankets, trying to block out the off-screen noises that sent chills down my spine. Her favorite was "A Nightmare on Elm Street"; I could never figure out if it was the fear of Freddy Krueger or her deep-rooted love for Johnny Depp that drove her fascination. For me, it was Leonardo DiCaprio who won me over as Romeo.

Wherefore art thou Romeo?

Yeah. Like I'd ever be lucky enough to be Claire Danes. She kissed *both* Leonardo DiCaprio *and* Jared Leto, who played Jordan Catalano, every nineties girl's crush.

I waver between wanting to contact him and the fear of what I might find if I do. It's been over twenty years since I last saw him. In the back of my mind, the urge to reach out is strong, but I'm unsure if I want to revisit the past. I'm intrigued by whatever he has to give me, though.

My mom knocks on my door, her voice soft and full of concern. Without waiting for an answer, she opens the door and steps inside. "Honey, I know you said you don't need to eat, but I made you a sandwich." The smell of toasted bread drifts through the air and I try to force out a smile. I love that she always toasts my bread.

"Thanks," I say in an even voice. Thoughts of Amy preoccupy my mind, yet I still accept the sandwich to make my mom happy. She worries enough already. Putting other people's needs ahead of my own seems to be a trait that I have developed over time.

Sometimes I can't help but feel like I'm losing a little of myself when I do so.

3

"A Tuesday meetup?" My friend Dani slides the monster Bloody Mary in front of me. The Copper Fig serves these giant drinks and they are oh-so good. "Something must be up."

Thursdays are my standing meetup with my besties at The Copper Fig. For years, we've gone every Thursday, only missing a Thursday here and there. Since Thanksgiving was last week, this is the first time we've seen each other in almost two weeks.

"No, nothing's up. I missed you all. How was everyone's Thanksgiving?"

"Well, you know how mine went because you were there," my sister Vivienne says, her words laced with both exasperation and amusement. "I just can't get away from you, can I?"

I smile and playfully shrug my shoulders. "Whatever. You love it. Besides, it's not like you'll see me *every* Thanksgiving. You said next year you're going to Cal's mom's."

Vivienne groans in response. "Don't remind me."

"I thought you two got along just fine now," Sadie says.

Vivienne tries her best to steer clear of conversations

involving Cal's mother. Initially, his mother disapproved of their relationship, but over time, she's started easing up on her disapproval. Nonetheless, the strain between them is evident.

"Yeah, we do, but it's still tough. Whenever I look at her, I can't help but think of how much she used to hate me. Nowadays, she works hard to be nice and welcoming—almost *too* hard."

"Hey, better she go overboard than be the bitch she was."

"Dani!" Dani speaks with a brusque frankness that can shock some people. She has no filter between her brain and her mouth. Her words sound harsh, and the people who don't know her are often taken aback. I know she means no ill will and speaks what she's thinking. Yet, I wish she would take a few moments to consider her audience and their feelings before speaking.

"Whatever," she says as she forms a W with her fingers on her forehead.

My gaze lingered on the jukebox near the back wall. I remember the day Amy's dad bought one for their house, how we danced around her living room to all the old tunes her parents played. The Beatles, Neil Diamond, The Jackson 5, Smokey Robinson. We'd dance until our sides ached.

Then Amy got sick, her life cut short within a year of her diagnosis. Within a month after that, Levi and his parents left town.

And now Levi has come back like a ghost in the night.

Sadie's hand crosses my vision like a shadow and snaps her fingers in front of my eyes. The sound breaks through the foggy thoughts, and I blink, finding her face right in front of mine. "Earth to Holly," she says. "You in there?"

"Sorry," I reply, shaking my head. "I was in a daze."

Vivienne nods knowingly. "What were you thinking about?"

I hesitate for a moment, then shake my head. "Nothing," I say softly, turning away from their concerned faces.

Dani throws a crumpled napkin in my direction, her features hardened with demand. "Come on. You can't leave us hanging. Spill it."

My sister and friends lean towards me, their eyes wide and expectant like a pack of hungry hounds waiting for a treat. While they are quiet, I feel their collective glare searing into my skin, the subtle pressure of their stares threatening to break me down.

I sigh, knowing I can never say no to them. They know my weaknesses better than anyone else—and aren't afraid of taking advantage of them.

"Fine."

"Yay!' The three of them cheer and exchange their high fives. They've broken me and are proud of it.

"Vivienne, do you remember Amy Walsh?" I ask, watching the memories behind her eyes spark to life.

"Oh my gosh, yes," Vivienne responds, her voice thick with emotion.

"What? Who is she?" Dani jumps in with a puzzled look on her face.

"Was," I reply, my voice heavy with grief. I drop my eyes to my drink and twist the straw between my fingers. "Up until age thirteen, she was my best friend. Then cancer took her." A lump rises in my throat as tears flood my eyes, and I take a deep breath to steady myself. Who would have thought that the very mention of Amy and her cancer could still bring me to tears after all these years?

Sadie's hand gently touches my back as her soft voice murmurs, "I'm so sorry." She gives me a few comforting rubs before turning to Viv and asking for more information. Viv's eyes turn distant as she retells the story of how Amy and I were like two peas in a pod until Amy passed away and her parents moved without a forwarding address. As Viv's words bounce around the room, I'm brought back to childhood memories of laughter and pizza in front of the television. "We never heard from them again," she says, finishing the story.

"Until now."

Viv's face fills with shock, and she instinctively spits out her drink, narrowly missing me. "What? They contacted you?"

I shake my head. "No. Not her parents. Levi. He sent me a letter."

Dani's expression changes from intrigue to confusion. "Who's Levi?"

"Amy's older brother," Viv replies. "We're the same age, but we didn't hang out or anything. Nice guy. What did his letter say, Holly?"

After taking a deep breath, I tell the story of Levi's letter, managing to relay it without breaking down into tears. As I explain everything, I almost can't believe it's true. "He gave me his phone number to call him if I want whatever he has."

Dani's fingertips drum on the table impatiently. "You're going to do it, right?"

"I don't know. I just received the letter yesterday. I haven't decided."

"Why wouldn't you?" Viv reaches her hand across the table and covers mine. "This is something from Amy. She'd want you to have whatever it is."

She's right. It's like having a piece of Amy, a part I so desperately wished I had when she left this Earth. "But what is it? Why wouldn't he just tell me? What if it's something crazy?"

"Like what?" Dani says. "You were thirteen. I'm sure it's something stupid like a lava lamp or a Caboodle."

"Speak for yourself. I still have my Caboodle." It's bright purple, detailed with teal accents and floral stickers I placed on the outside through the years. Some may think it's odd I keep my makeup in it, but it's practical and a reminder of simpler times. "I'm just scared of what he has to give me."

"Is he cute? Maybe he'll give you more than you think."

"Dani! Let's not make this about sex, okay? You have a one-track mind." Dani chuckles, and then I continue. "I'm afraid of what bringing up the past might do. That's why I'm hesitant." Though simply receiving the letter has stirred up emotions I thought I'd dealt with long ago.

Viv's hand rests on my shoulder as she speaks with a gentleness that only a loving older sister can have. "Sweetie, I know it might be difficult, but it also may be nice seeing Levi again." Her golden eyes are filled with understanding, and I know she's right.

I owe so much to Viv. When I was younger, she took me to the side of the driveway where my little pink bike was, steading me as I wobbled out of the safety of my training wheels. On the first day of middle school, she was late to her first class as she walked me to mine. And when Amy died, she tucked me into bed and laid down on the hardwood floor next to my bed for two weeks, whispering quiet words of comfort until I drifted off to sleep. Viv has been a rock for me throughout my life, always there when I need her.

Vivienne is more than a sister. She's my best friend.

"He reached out to you, Holly. Even though whatever he has may end up being nothing big, it's obviously important to him that he gives it to you." Sadie tilts her head to the side and fixes her gaze upon me. "Besides, maybe this Levi guy is what you need right now."

"Don't start with me," I say as I roll my eyes and take a deep breath. "You think this is a sign, don't you?"

Sadie nods her head eagerly and widens her eyes. It seems everything is a sign to her—the way she met her husband, Joe; the birth of their daughter, Rose; and the boost Viv got with her business after playing an origami fortune teller game. It had even been a sign that pushed Viv into the arms of Cal, her boyfriend. She calls it being in tune with the universe.

Divorcing my husband and having my credit score ruined by his gambling addiction was an painful blow I could have never imagined the universe would bring me. We have different ideas of how the universe works.

It seems to be against me.

"What? You don't know. It *could* be a sign. Don't be so quick to dismiss it."

"I also don't need to be involved right now. That's what you're thinking, Dani, that I can hook up with Levi. That's *so* not where my mind is right now, and I highly doubt that's where his mind is, either. We haven't seen each other in years. Besides, you all agreed I needed to take a break from dating when I brought that loser to poker that night."

"That was ages ago! I did love kicking surfer boy out of my condo, though." Dani touches her finger above her lip and thumb beneath her chin, recalling the night she demanded my guest leave after being a dick to me.

That's the thing about us being so close. We won't let anyone hurt each other. Not if we can help it.

"It's so busy at work, though. And I'm trying to keep my cool with Scottie. I don't know if I even have time to meet with Levi." That's the honest-to-God truth. I'm exhausted by the time I finish work. I barely have time to pee. Thanks to Owen, I'm working so much overtime to try and pay all my debt.

"You had time to meet us!"

"Yeah, but you guys are my best friends. I'll always make time for you."

"Aw," Dani says, "we love you, too. Now, I see a cute guy over there, and he's been looking my way for the past five minutes."

"What? Are you going to leave to talk to that guy? He looks like"—Viv turns around, glances at the guy, and turns back to us with her mouth dropped open—"Brad Pitt. So, yeah, go ahead. Leave. We're cool with that."

"Thanks, gals." Dani hops off her chair, takes money out of her pocket, and tosses it onto the table. "Don't wait up."

"How does she do it?" I inquire. "She has no filter, no fear. She sees something and goes for it. Usually a guy, but even her career." Three months ago, she gave notice at her human resources job, and now she's a full-time photographer. She had a dream and made it work. Heck, the same goes for Sadie, whose dream of becoming a vice-principal has now come true, and my sister who has achieved her long-time goal of opening a store for her business.

Here I am practically living paycheck to paycheck due to my poor choice of men.

"You can, too, Holly. We believe in you, and you have to believe in yourself more. You're so awesome, and you don't even know it. You should meet this Levi guy and see what your friend left for you. It may provide closure you didn't know you needed."

"That's the vice-principal coming out of you. Do you give that speech to all your students?"

"Tell them to go meet guys? I manage a middle school, so no." Sadie laughs. "I believe it, though. And you should, too."

I turn back toward Dani, who is chatting it up with the gentleman she pointed out earlier. It may be time to step out of my comfort zone.

❧ 4 ❧

s soon as I walk into the coffee shop, the aroma of fresh coffee beans fills my senses and sends a calming effect through me. I need this right now.

I nervously glance at the clock behind the barista's counter, counting down until Levi is due to arrive. I'm tempted to ditch the meet-up and race back home. The week has been long, though, and while I'm a bit antsy about seeing Levi, I think catching up with a cup of coffee may be a good thing.

I close my eyes as I inhale the aroma of freshly brewed coffee, giving me a little extra boost of energy. I grab a mug, line up the barcode on my phone with the scanner and pour myself a cup. I love that this café has a self-serve area. I take a sip, and my mouth waters at the thought of pairing this with a warm piece of pie.

Before I can consider the pie any further, a handsome man enters the café. There is no doubt in my mind; it's Levi. He's exactly as I remember him, but older. He is tall, which he has always been, with dark hair and brilliant blue eyes. His square jaw makes his face look like a Ken doll. From the smile on his face, it is clear that he recognizes me, too.

"Holly!" he exclaims, walking over. "It's been a long time." He gives me a warm hug, and I can't help but smile. I'm still shocked that he is here after all these years.

"H-hi," I stutter, my eyes darting around the room, my face reddening. I hold my coffee mug high in the air so I don't spill it as he hugs me tighter.

He releases his hug and steps back. "I can't believe how many years it's been."

His voice cracks, and I feel the weight of his words in my stomach. "I know. Hard to believe, right?" I force a laugh in an attempt to lighten the mood. "We're like grown-ups now."

The moment my words hang in the air, I want to take them back. Of course we're grown-ups—mature adults—not awkward teenagers. Why did I let my "friends" talk me into meeting him? I'm making a fool of myself.

"Should we sit?" Levi gestures toward a small round table nestled in the corner of the shop, its top surface reflecting the bright light shining through the nearby window.

"Yeah, sure. You want anything?"

"Um, I guess coffee is fine. Is it self-serve, or are you in the habit of taking what you want whenever you want it?"

He smiles, his eyes crinkling at the corners. Had he seen me through the window when I got my coffee?

"Specialty drinks you order from the baristas. If you're after black coffee, they have a self-serve station."

"Good. For a minute, I thought you were a thief."

"Nope. Not a chance. I'm not that interesting. However, you do use your phone to pay if you use self-serve. I have their app on my phone. I've got this."

"Thanks." He looks at the label above the percolator outlining the prices. "A buck twenty. How can I ever repay you?"

He's the same Levi I remember, delivering his words with a hint of sarcasm behind them. Could it be that reuniting with him is as simple as slipping on an old, comfortable pair of shoes?

After grabbing his coffee, we sit at the table he pointed out before. I wrap my hands around my mug and look down at the rising steam. Amy's smiling face pops into my mind and sends a pang of sadness through my heart. The silence between us stretches like an endless void. I try to think of something to say, but all I can find are words of sorrow.

He licks his lips and smiles nervously. "It's been a long time. What are you doing now? Married? Kids? Are you a senator yet?"

I let out a short laugh. "What? A senator? What gave you that idea?"

"Your dad is a politician, right? I thought you'd follow in his footsteps."

There had been a time it crossed my mind. Being involved in local government kept my dad super busy, so much that it took a lot of time away from Vivienne and me. That was about as far as my interest went. "No. He's not in politics anymore, though. He hurt his hip last year and retired. Now he keeps busy at home."

"Do you live near your parents?"

My pulse throbbed in my veins as I considered how to approach my answer. How do I tell him I'm a grown woman living with my parents?

"Hello?" Levi says after I've been quietly thinking about my response. "Do you not know if you live near them? Near constitutes maybe a ten or fifteen-minute drive."

There's that sarcasm again. "Yeah, I know what it means. Actually, I live with them right now." I don't have a reason to lie, as embarrassing as it is that I live with them. I'm not trying to impress Levi. I came for whatever it is he wants to give me. That's it. More than likely, I won't see him again after today.

"Oh? Are you helping out with your dad?" He sips his coffee.

That seems like a valid assumption based on my dad hurting his hip and retiring. Levi sees me as the good daughter who gave up her independence to take care of someone she loves. Unfortunately, that's not even close to the truth.

"I'm divorced. My ex put us in so much debt that I'm staying with them until I can get back on my feet." Brief, to the point, and not likely to encourage more questions. People don't like discussing money, so the mention of Owen putting me in financial ruin is enough to squash that out of the conversation.

Levi smiles. "That's totally understandable. I'm sure your parents are happy to have you around."

His words make me feel a little better, and I return his smile. "You think?"

"Definitely. You can help them out whenever they need it, and you can see them every day. I'd give anything to see my mom again. Amy, too."

"I didn't think of it that way." I'm such a jerk thinking how bad it looks living with my parents at my age, and here he's lost so much and would love to be in my situation.

"I'm sure you miss your privacy, though."

I let out a heavy sigh as I run my fingers along the back of my neck, trying to massage away the tension. Stress had taken a toll on my body, making me lose weight, and my muscles ache. "Yeah. Sometimes. My mom is always pressuring me about something or another."

"I do remember that. She'd come knocking on our door to remind you to do the dishes. Or sign the card for your Aunt

Barb's birthday because the mailman was down the street, and she had to get it in the mailbox."

I roll my eyes in exasperation. "It's always something with her, and it hasn't changed," I say.

"Your mom is great, though. Amy really liked her," Levi says.

At the mention of Amy's name, I feel all the color drain from my face. Levi's mouth opens before he quickly stops himself from speaking, obviously aware of the effect his words have on me.

"Levi, I'm so sorry about Amy." My voice cracks.

"No, Holly. *I'm* sorry. My parents packed up the house in a matter of days without giving me a chance to say goodbye. With Amy's passing, my mom was desperate for a change of scenery and thought that leaving would help her heal faster from the pain."

My eyes grow warm, and a lump forms in my throat as I press my palm to my chest. Memories of me and Amy's family flood my mind. We'd ride our bikes around the neighborhood, swim at the local pool, and go to the park for picnics. But then, suddenly, Amy was gone, and then her family. All that was left was an empty house, an empty yard, and my broken heart.

Yes, I had lost my best friend. But Levi's parents had lost a *child*. Everywhere they went, people offered condolences, and their faces filled with pity. His mom didn't want to forget Amy, but she didn't want a daily reminder that she wouldn't see her only daughter become a grown woman.

"That makes perfect sense. I'm so sorry about everything."

"You say that like you're the reason she got sick. Nothing we say can change what happened." He pauses for a minute, and sadness sweeps over his face.

"So, do you have any kids? Married?" My eyes bounce to his hand, where I don't see a ring.

"Not married." He wiggles his bare ring finger at me. "I never found the right person." His stare lingers for a moment. "Maybe someday."

Heat crawls up my neck as our eyes lock. The spell between us breaks when a cup nearby clatters to the ground. "So about these things you have of Amy's?"

"Yeah!" He opens his jacket and pulls out an envelope, handing it to me. The envelope is sealed. I run my fingers over the ink on the front. My name and address in Amy's handwriting. Seeing this, her voice floods into my head like a tidal wave. I can hear her yelling, "Ready or not, here I come!" when we play hide and seek, and her whispering secrets in my ear during Social Studies when Mr. Drexel wasn't paying attention.

I burst into tears in the middle of the coffee shop. I don't think I've ever cried in public. Not even at Amy's funeral. I was too shocked over her being gone.

"I'm sorry," I wipe my face with my arm. "I don't know where that came from."

"I do." Levi reaches across the table and puts his hand over mine. The touch startles me, though I find it warm and comforting. "There are times it still hits me out of nowhere."

I sob more when he says this, the sudden guilt of not thinking about Amy for years crashing into me like the waves of Lake Michigan. "I should have tried to find you guys after you left."

"How? You were thirteen, Holly. It's not like we had advanced internet searches or anything at that time. There wasn't Facebook or Instagram or anything to easily find someone. Besides, my parents didn't exactly want to be found." He pulls his hand from mine and rests it on the table.

"When we moved, it was like Amy never existed. We were a family of three. Just like that." He snaps his fingers.

I look away, unsure of what to say. Nothing I say can comfort him. I know this.

"Look at us, a couple of depressed people sitting and having coffee."

A smirk forms on his face as he rubs his thumb on the handle of his coffee mug. "Yeah, we're the cheeriest people on the planet." He reaches back into his jacket pocket. "There's something else, too."

My heart stops when he presents a cheap, plastic charm necklace. I take it from him, my hand visibly shaking.

"I...I haven't seen this for years." The blue chain link, flimsy at best, holds a barrage of colorful charms hooked through each loop. A yellow tennis racket, a pink skateboard, red baseball bat with ball, and a blue hairdryer. We played some game at the local fair—I can't recall which one—and won it. We'd find a charm at a general store every few months and add to it. She had it last. I had asked her for it so I could wear it to the eighth-grade dance, but she passed away before she had an opportunity to give it back to me.

"It was hidden away, tucked between a bookshelf and the wall like she didn't want anyone to find it or maybe was keeping it safe. I held onto it for all these years, but I think you should have it."

The tears I finally had gotten control over start again. They're running down my cheeks, dripping onto the table. I sniffle. "Wow."

"I remember teasing Amy about how corny it was, but she loved it, treating it like a diamond necklace or something."

"There's another charm to put on it. A deep yellow boom box with a red handle. I was next to have it and put a charm on."

"Well, now you can."

He says this so matter-of-factly, so confident that she left this on purpose for me and that this is what I need for closure. It's not, though. This opens up so many more feelings.

I let the charms dangle from my hand, touching and outlining each one with my finger. "I'll have to find the charm. I honestly don't know what I did with it." I hate that. I should know exactly where the charm is. But moving from my parent's house to my college dorm to my first apartment to my place with Owen and then back to my parent's house— wow, that's a lot of moving—it has to be around in a box I haven't opened yet.

"I think you'll find it."

He's so confident about this. Me, not so much.

"I should get going." I don't have anywhere to be, but the more I sit here with Levi, the more I miss Amy. And I want to start my search for this charm. "If you don't mind, I'll open this letter at home."

"No, please do. I have no idea what's in it. Maybe it's one of those chain letters. I remember her telling me she wrote you a letter before… " He trails off, unable to complete the sentence, but I know the words he means to say.

"It was nice seeing you. And thank you for this. I really appreciate it." I place the letter and necklace in my purse.

"No problem. And thank you for the dollar twenty coffee." He shifts the mug toward me. "Maybe I'll buy you a cup next time."

"Oh." I didn't anticipate a next time. Is he planning on making this a regular thing? "Okay, sure."

"I gather from that reaction you don't intend on seeing me again."

"It's not that, it's just—" I don't have a reason. There is nothing to say. All I'm trying to do is process what's happening right now.

"I understand. It's a shock to your system seeing me after so many years. No pressure." He tips back his mug and downs the rest of his coffee. "You have my number. Text me if you're interested in some more coffee." He taps his knuckles on the table, stands up, and walks out the door.

I'm only surviving today if someone sticks a coffee-filled IV in me. I'm running on intermittent sleep. I kept Amy's letter next to my bed, and every hour or so, I'd wake up, contemplate reading it, and then change my mind. All night was like this.

Why am I so terrified of what's inside?

I brought the letter to work today in case I muster up the courage to read it. The more I think about it, the more I'm convinced it's a chain letter. If I read it, I'll be stuck with the burden of sending eight copies within ten days or face dire consequences. Gosh, Amy loved chain letters.

A chill runs through me as I stand in the cramped, dimly lit room. I'm grateful I had the foresight to keep a sweater here, as the frigid temperature makes me feel like I'm standing in a freezer. This room is like an oven in the summer, but in the winter, it feels like a different world entirely. I'm so cold I feel like my nipples could cut through ice.

I shrug my sweater on and fold the sleeves over each

other. I hug myself and take a deep breath. Now is as good a time as ever to read whatever this is.

My grip is so firmly on the envelope I'm afraid it may disintegrate right in my hands. It's hard to believe how sweaty my palms are, considering how cold it is in this room. I turn the envelope around and start tearing it open.

"Knock, knock." Nora Traves, one of my best employees, startles me. "Can I talk to you for a second?"

"Sure!" I toss the envelope down, wondering when and if I'll ever read what is inside. I put on my happy face because that's who I am. I'm pretty sure Scottie is the only person I can't fake a smile for. "Have a seat. I don't have an extra jacket, or I'd offer one."

"I'm fine, thanks." She sits down. "I can stand a few minutes in this room. I don't know how you spend more than a half hour at a time in here, though." She's wearing a short-sleeve shirt under her work vest, and the goose pimples dot up and down her arms.

"Trust me." I click a pen open and closed. "I try not to. The less time I'm in here, the better. What can I do for you?"

As I fold my hands on the table and lean in to give her my undivided attention, she bites her lower lip to the point she's chewing on it.

"Nora, talk to me. You know I have an open-door policy." I take that seriously. I had a situation with a male classmate in college that my instructor refused to address. Eventually, I had to take it to the dean. I swore I'd always be someone who listened to others.

She shifts in the chair and clears her throat. "It's about Scottie."

I hold in a grunt. It's *always* about Scottie. I can't seem to find it in myself to fire him. If I do that, I may lose my job. I'm in too much debt for that to happen.

"I don't like to be a snitch or anything." She trails off and rubs her hands on her khakis. I'm not too fond of the khakis we have to wear. They are company issued, though, along with our maroon vests. Does anyone look good in a vest?

"Don't worry about it. If something's going on, I need to know about it." I appreciate her not wanting to be labeled a tattletale, but this isn't first grade, and I'm sure she's not telling on him for chewing gum in class.

"Okay. Well, the thing is, I came in early this morning. I walked past the liquor section and saw Scottie pocket some little bottles of wine. You know, the one-serving size ones." She uses her thumb and forefinger to mimic the size.

"Yes, I'm aware of them." Sometimes I buy them when I have the girls over. I used to anyway when I had a place of my own. "You're saying he stole them?"

"Yes. Well, I think so." She bites her lip again, and her eyes move up toward the ceiling. "I'm not positive, but I'm pretty sure. He was putting them in his jacket. I didn't see a bag or a receipt or anything."

"Okay. Thank you for the information, Nora. I appreciate it." Another strike for Scottie. He's making it so hard for me to hold on to him. Even if I fire him, his mom will fire me and then probably give him his job back.

This completely sucks.

"Is he going to get in trouble?"

"I'm not sure yet. I'll speak with him. Thank you for bringing this to my attention."

She leaves the room, and I lay my head on the desk. I hate this part of my job. Do I think Scottie stole the wine? Yeah. More than likely. He fits the profile. Can I prove it? I have no idea. And what if he didn't do it? I don't want to assume the worst of Scottie. It's *possible* he has a decent side, that he's not a completely despicable human being.

Nah.

I look over at the envelope again—enough with the waiting. I need to tear open this letter and read it before I lose the nerve to do that, too.

I get up from my desk and slowly shut the door, locking it for extra measure. I turn off the overhead light—I can use my desk lamp. No one will see a light under the door and bother me while I read it.

I scoot the chair in and close my eyes as I take a deep breath. Before I open the envelope, I study the writing for a moment. I laugh. We used to write notes all day during school, folding them up like little footballs and our hands meeting in the middle as we passed them to each other. On the first day of school, we always sat next to each other to claim our desks.

I'm careful as I slide my finger underneath the envelope's seal. I want to save the envelope, so I don't want to damage it. Once the envelope is open, I pinch the paper with my fingers. I pull it out and set it on the desk.

This is it. I can't put it off any longer.

I unfold the paper and set it on the desk to read it like it's so fragile it may break if I hold it. Not only has she written a letter, but cute hearts and stars are drawn all over it. She loved drawing and dreamed of becoming a children's book illustrator. She would have been amazing at it, too.

Here goes nothing:

Holly,

It's weird seeing my handwriting and hearing from me after so much time, isn't it? I'm sure you're reading this sometime in the future. Maybe one year, ten years. Oh my gosh, what if it's like 20 years, and you're married to Marky Mark and have five kids? Snarky Sam, Bouncy Billy, Pretty Pam, Funny Frank, and Jumpy Jane?

I'm wiping tears before they fall onto the paper and smear her words. She always made me laugh, and yes, I had a very unhealthy crush on Marky Mark. She wouldn't believe what a huge actor Mark Wahlberg has become!

Whatever time it is, I hope you're healthy, successful, and happy. I'm sorry I'm not there with you. I'm sorry I got sick. It wasn't supposed to be this way.

You've been the most amazing friend. Sure, we've had some big fights, but what friends don't have that? I don't know what happens when you die, but I hope you can still feel my presence and know how much I love you.

This may sound crazy, but Levi can't really get mad at me since I won't be around. My brother has a massive crush on you. He thinks I don't know, but I see how he looks at you. He's in high school now, so I think he's afraid to admit it. Give him time. I'm sure he'll finally tell you by the time you are in high school or college. I think you like him, too. I've caught you stealing glances at him. I want to tell you I'm okay with that, Holly. Just think, if I were around, maybe you could BE my sister by this point. Gosh, that would be amazing.

I have to go now. I'm getting pretty tired, so I need to rest. I'll make sure you get this somehow after I'm gone.

I love you, Holly. You're my best friend always and forever.

Love,

Amy

I turn my head and take a breath. I want nothing more than to wrap her in a big hug, which isn't possible. God, I miss her so much.

Levi had a crush on me? I hadn't a clue, and I'm not sure how I feel about that. Either way, between this and the necklace, I'm feeling connected to her in a way I haven't since before she passed away. There's a lot to unpack in this last letter I'll ever have from her.

I need that last charm to complete this necklace. I fold the letter back up and slide it into the envelope. I'll find that charm if it's the last thing I do.

❧ 6 ❧

A nother day, another dollar. That's the saying, and it's my life right now. Work, sleep, and repeat. Every penny I have goes toward food and my car payment. Every week I allot fifty dollars for my Thursday night get-together with Dani, Sadie, and Viv. The rest goes toward debt payoff. I'll get there; I know I will. It just seems like I'll be living in a retirement home by the time that happens.

I'm running on no sleep today. Amy's letter is tattooed on my brain. Every time I close my eyes, I picture her handwriting and every word she wrote. I almost have the letter memorized by this point. After perhaps a total of about four hours of intermittent sleep, I'm staring at the start of an eight-hour workday.

It'll be a miracle if I make it through today without snapping at someone.

I sigh as I hang up my jacket, thinking about how today I have to talk to Scottie about Nora's claims. And by talk, I mean tiptoe around it. Without any solid proof, I can't start throwing accusations around. Theft fits Scottie's character, and I'm sure he's likely guilty, but his mom owns the store.

There's no need to waste any time. I should speak with him right away. I check the clock on my phone, and it's 8:07. He should be here by now, and I swear I saw his car, a junky pine green Saturn, in the parking lot. I stop by the security room but don't see him there.

Before requesting him on the intercom, I peek down the aisle, one by one, searching for him. I realize I've passed him in the pasta aisle, so I backtrack. He's flirting with Hilary Grand, one of the floor associates. She's three years older than him and puts up with his constant flirting. I've offered to speak with him about it, but she said she isn't bothered by it.

Why is it that I don't take issue with a conversation regarding his flirtatious ways with Hilary, but I'm practically quivering when it comes to theft?

They're both terrible things and need addressing.

"Excuse me, Scottie?" I step toward him, and Hilary waves and rushes away, more than likely happy for the interruption. Scottie crosses his arms and leans against a shelf.

"What's up, boss?"

I hate when he acts super casual like this. I don't bother saying anything anymore, though. It's easier to accept his quirks, as annoying as they are, so I can make it through my day. There are more important things to worry about, like employees stealing alcohol.

"Can we chat in my office?"

He shifts his weight and darts his eyes from left to right. "I have to get back to work. Can we chat here real quick?"

This tells me he knows he's caught. My office is a forty-five-second walk from aisle eight. I won't have such a serious conversation between corkscrew noodles on one side and garlic-flavored sauce on the other. And if he has time to flirt with Hilary, he certainly has time to discuss this possible theft issue in my office.

"No." I turn, start leaving the aisle, and realize he's not behind me.

I turn around, and he's still leaning against the shelf, picking at his fingernails. "Scottie? Let's go."

He shakes his head and pushes off the shelf, a few boxes of rotini crashing to the ground. "Sorry, boss." He picks them up and returns them to their places. Admittedly, I'm shocked he did.

"My office. *Now*." This time I'm stern with him, so he knows I'm not kidding around or putting up with anything. I turn on my heel and march to my office; this time, he's following behind.

When we reach my office, I shut the door behind him and sit at the desk. He sits across from me.

"Are you having a nice morning, Miss James?"

His fake small talk makes me want to throw up. He's an Eddie Haskell all the way. "It's fine, thank you. I need to speak with you about something." I fold my hands and set them on my desk, heat rising in my chest. "I'm going to come out and ask. Did you take wine from the store without paying?"

"You're asking me if I stole wine? I'm not even old enough to drink!"

He says this as though I don't know that. "I know. You're nineteen. That's the other issue. But one infraction at a time. Tell me the truth. Did you do it?"

"Hell no, I didn't do it."

"Scottie, there's no need for foul language." I'm lax on many things, but he's being very disrespectful, and I'm not having it right now.

"Whatever." He waves his hand at me.

"You *are* aware that I can simply check the cameras, right?" I don't want to have to do that. I want him to do the right thing and come clean.

"You have to submit a request for that, Miss James."

I curl my lips into a small smile. "Not in the case of a theft. If I believe there was a theft, I can look now and submit paperwork later."

His face falls, and even in the windowless room, I can see his face turn white. "I'm not saying I did anything, but if I *did,* what would happen?"

"Well," I unfold my hands and straighten some of the papers on my desk, making him wait and sweat a moment. "There are a few options. First, I can report you to the police for theft and underage drinking. Second, I can fire you."

He fixes his gaze on me with a challenging look. "You wouldn't."

I don't respond, keeping my eyes on him. He needs to know I'm serious, even if I'm not sure if I am.

"Fine. I took the wine. I won't do it again, I promise. Please don't tell my mom."

He's *begging* me. The only thing missing is him on his knees with his hands folded. As much as I'd enjoy that, I can't let greed take over.

There has to be a way for me to avoid involving his mother. I want to punish him, but I want to keep my job, too. "Here's what we're going to do. You're going to pay the store back for the wine you took. You're also going to stop bothering Hilary. She's not interested in you, and you shouldn't be trying to pick up women during your working hours, anyway. Do this, and I won't tell your mother. However, if I catch you again, I'll tell your mother, fire you, and call the police."

I'm so firm in this belief that I almost scare myself with my tone. Scottie's gone from slouching in the chair to a straight spine, listening to my every word. "Thank you, Miss James."

I nod and dismiss him from my office. The second he

shuts the door, I exhale, as though I'd been holding my breath for years.

7

I hug my knees to my chest and slowly rock back and forth on my bed as Dani holds the necklace, inspecting each charm.

"Wow, Holly. This is phenomenal. Think about it. After all these years, you have this piece of your friend back. You must feel incredible."

Sliding my legs back out, I push my back against the headboard. "I don't know how I feel, to be honest. I haven't thought about Amy in so many years. This is a lot to take in."

Dani hands the necklace back to me. "You know what Sadie would say, don't you?"

I roll my eyes, knowing all too well. "This is complete fate, the universe telling me something. It's like she's never heard of a coincidence."

"It's neat, though, how she reads into this stuff. I mean, we don't know. Maybe there *is* some magical force determining our paths. I'm not religious, but this happens after all these years. Maybe it *does* mean something."

The thought *had* crossed my mind. The idea of Amy somehow making this happen brings joy to my heart, proof that even though she is not physically here, she is not really gone. "Do you want to see the letter she wrote me?"

When I first read it, I vowed to keep it to myself. Dani is one of my best friends though, and I want my friends to know about Amy.

Dani takes her time reading the letter. I can place precisely where she is as she reads, since I have memorized almost every word.

"Hello?" she says as she waves the letter in her hand. "Why didn't you show me this first, lady? Forget signs. This isn't a sign. It's a billboard."

"What?" I hop off the bed and sit in my bay window, embracing the change of scenery. My bedroom window overlooks the street, and while the leaves are almost off the trees, the golds and reds remaining are breathtaking.

"Holly, this dude has a thing for you."

"*Had*. That was over twenty years ago. This isn't Joe and Sadie." Joe and Sadie's relationship played out like a fairytale romance. She crushed on him for years in school, and it wasn't until just recently that they found each other again.

"No, it's not. This is your story, Holly, and I'm convinced he found you not only to give you Amy's letter but because of what's *in* this letter."

As usual, Dani has missed the point, putting her focus on the male aspect of this story. "This letter, the necklace, it's not about Levi." I leave my place of solace and snatch the necklace off the bed. "This is about closure, and with this necklace, maybe I can finally have that. I have to find the last charm I bought to put it on. That will complete it. Make it final." Dani embraces me as I start sobbing.

"Shh." She strokes my hair. "It's okay. We'll find it. I promise."

I strengthen my hold on her. "I miss her so much." Had I allowed myself to cry like this when Amy passed away? I don't know. What I *do* know is that I need these tears more than I need air right now.

"I know, and I'm sorry for not focusing on Amy and how much you miss her. Should we start looking for the charm? Why waste time?"

I pull away and wipe my eyes. "We don't have to." I doubt she wants to stick around and search through my unpacked boxes and anywhere else I could have it hidden away.

"Yes, we do." Dani spins around in the room. "Let's start in the closet."

"We'll never find it. It's so little, like searching for a needle in a haystack."

"Well, it's a good thing my grandfather owned a farm. Let's get to it." She claps her hands together as she swings open the closet door, removes one of the many unlabeled boxes, and plops it onto my bed. "Let's get started."

We spend the next hour searching through boxes, pulling every single item out. While I'm not convinced we will find anything, I appreciate that Dani is so willing to do this with me. I even create a pile of items to throw away, which will make my mom happy. She hates clutter, and I brought plenty of it with me when I moved back in.

"Do you have any boxes at the storage facility?"

When I moved back home, I put some excess items, like furniture and small appliances, in a storage unit. I haven't been there in a while, but I don't recall many boxes being there. "I can look there, too."

"What about the basement?"

I shake my head. "More than likely not. Once it flooded, we cleared everything out. Any boxes that weren't damaged, I moved up here." Clean-up took a few weeks, and I don't even know what I lost. What if the charm had been in one of those boxes? If I can't find it, I can only assume that's the case. And then I will *never* have any closure. I skip past the thought, not wanting to deal with it unless I have no other choice. Right now, I need to remain positive.

"I have an idea." Dani races out of my room, and I follow her. She corners my mom in the kitchen.

"Mrs. James, do you know if Holly has any boxes elsewhere? Maybe in the garage?"

My mom wipes her hands on the towel she's holding and places it on the counter. "I don't believe so. What are you two up to?"

"Nothing, Mom. We're searching for something."

"What? Maybe I can help."

The extra set of eyes would certainly be helpful, but I don't want to bring this up with her. I'm doing this on my own. I love my mom, but I don't need her to be a part of everything. Living with her again has taken away some of my personal space.

"A charm. She had a charm for a necklace and can't find it."

"Charm?" My mom's smile falls. "The last time I heard about a charm necklace was when you were about thirteen."

The somber tone in her voice gives away she's remembering Amy. She knows how much that necklace meant to me. While some friends had broken best friends' necklaces, we had this. My mom hated how I shut her out after Amy died, refusing to talk to her or see a therapist. I was a teenager dealing with, or rather avoiding, the death of my best friend. How I reacted was not her fault, but I know she feels like she wished she had done more.

"Do you remember Levi?" I ask my mom. "Amy's brother? He had the necklace and gave it to me. I want to find the charm I didn't get to put on it."

She presses her hand to her chest. "You heard from Levi? Oh my, it's been so many years. When did this happen?"

"I met him for coffee the other day. He's doing well. His

mom passed away, and his dad is moving into a nursing home in town."

"Oh no. That's terrible about his mom." She ponders this for a moment. "And wow, Jerry is my age. He's going into a nursing home?"

My mom has difficulty processing growing older, especially after my dad's hip surgery. She's always thought of them as active and young at heart. Overall, their health is good. She struggles when she learns of people her age passing away or needing assistance.

"He didn't give me a lot of details. We mostly talked about Amy and this necklace. Do you have any idea where the charm could be?"

"I don't, honey. I'll make sure to keep my eyes peeled, though."

I'm sure she will, but the more I think about where this charm could be, I realize I know the answer.

And it's the worst possible place ever.

8

"What am I going to do?" I rub my hands against my face, pushing my fists into my eyes. "I can't go there."

When speaking with my mom, I realized of all the places the charm can be, that it's likely still with Owen. My ex-husband. The gambler. The one I don't have a relationship with anymore. That was one of the good things about us never having kids, no matter how much I wanted them. Now that we're divorced, I can completely cut him off and never have to see him again.

Although now, if I want that charm, I don't have a choice. My stomach lurches at the thought.

I call an emergency gathering with Dani, Viv, and Sadie at The Copper Fig. Sadie can't make it because Rose has an ear infection, the poor girl. She's almost eighteen months old and seems to get those a lot.

"Are you positive it's with Owen? I thought you did a pretty good job cleaning out all your stuff. I can go with you to the storage unit to help you look." Viv's offer is nice, but I'm sure it's not there.

I shake my head. "Positive. I don't even have any boxes there. It's all furniture. If the charm is in the apartment, I don't know where. I did a pretty thorough job packing my stuff, but I obviously missed it. It could be shoved back in a drawer, stuck behind a cabinet, or maybe he even threw it away for all I know." God, I hope that isn't true. If he did throw it away, I don't know what I'll do. I'm sure *I* never threw it away. I wouldn't have done that.

"I can go with you," Dani says as she pushes up her sleeves. "If he messes with you, I can take him."

She brings a smile to my face, which I desperately need. "No, it's fine. I can do it. I *should* do it. I haven't spoken with Owen since the divorce. He was in a pretty bad place when I left."

Leaving Owen was both the easiest and most challenging thing I have ever had to do. I loved him, I really did, but his addiction destroyed our marriage. I wanted it to work, but I couldn't allow him to ruin my life *and* credit. So I gathered up every ounce of strength I had and left.

Maybe that's what makes the thought of seeing him so suffocating.

"I'm sure it's hard. Remember when Jack showed up at my apartment?"

Viv reminds me of the fall when her ex, Jack, moved back to the United States after living in London for many years. They were practically engaged when he left, and their relationship fizzled. Then he came back and tried to start their relationship again. She refused, partly because she had moved on with her now boyfriend, Cal, but mostly because she knew their relationship wouldn't work.

"I do. That must have been so weird."

"It was, but it also gave me some closure, something I'm not sure you have. For me, to stand in front of Jack and not feel anything was amazing. It assured me I had made the right decision. You know you made the right choice, but maybe seeing him will help you close that chapter of your life."

Closing a chapter of my life feels so final—finish the book, put it on the shelf, and start the next volume.

ONE HOUR AND THREE DRINKS LATER, WE'RE IN STITCHES at our little round table in the corner of the bar. We always start at the bar, but we come together at the table. It's like a ritual; the bar is our meeting place, and the table, our sanctuary.

Viv leaps out of her chair and begins to dance enthusiastically when "Baby, Baby, Baby" by TLC comes on (RIP Lisa "Left Eye" Lopes). She sings along to Chili's parts of the song. "This is my jam!" she exclaims as I sense people's eyes drawn toward us.

"Come on, now, sit down." I point to her chair. Everyone here doesn't need to be looking at us, judging us.

No matter how much I beg her to stop, she only sings louder and sways her hips even more. I'm out of here without a second thought if she starts twerking.

Viv sits down when I cover my face with my hands. "Party pooper."

"I'm not a party pooper. I just don't want anyone to know I'm here with you."

"Stop it. You love TLC, and you know it."

Growing up, I always loved the music I was surrounded by, but looking back now, some of the lyrics I was singing along to flew right over my head! It's pretty amusing to realize that certain songs my parents let me listen to were actually quite risqué. Nonetheless, I still love them! "Tell me, Viv, do you require plenty of conversation with your sex, as the song suggests?" I used to listen to "Baby, Baby, Baby" on repeat.

"My lips are sealed." She pretends to lock her lips and throw away the key.

Now that she's stopped making me cringe at her singing and awkward dancing, I can finally start thinking about other things.

"What am I going to do, guys?"

"I thought you decided to go see Owen," Dani says before taking a swig of her beer.

"That, yes, but I mean this crippling debt. The grocery store isn't cutting it. I've had three drinks tonight, and that's it. That's all I'm able to do until I get paid again. I have no money to go out. Everything I make goes to pay off debt because of Owen. I need a part-time gig or something better than what I have now."

"Gosh, Holly, I knew it was bad, but is it *that* terrible?"

"Do you think I'd be living with Mom and Dad if things were *good*? I want—no, need—to get out of their house already." I glare at Viv.

Dani digs into the community plate of fries on our table. She hasn't eaten anything like that for a while. Her celiac disease has been under control for some time now. I hope she doesn't regret eating this later. "Is there anything else you can do? Like, what are your talents?"

I shrug. "You've got me. I've been stuck at the grocery store for so long I can't even remember what my degree is in."

"Graphic design, Holly. Why haven't you done anything with that?"

The world of graphic design has changed so much since I graduated from college. I loved drawing just as Amy did, though she preferred the children-like illustrations. I always thought it'd be neat to work in animation. Maybe draw on some big cartoon or something. When I graduated, I took the first job I could, which happened to be at the grocery store. I've been there ever since.

"You've been working at that store for over fifteen years. Aren't you sick of it?"

"Of course, Dani. It's the same thing day in and day out. I'm dealing with punks like Scottie. I thought by now I'd be drawing awesome characters, not shelving toilet paper." I'm a failure in every sense of the word. The only one in my family who isn't successful.

"There's nothing wrong in working in the industry you are," Viv reminds me. "Whether you realize it or not, your job is important."

"I know. And there are days I love it. I guess I just pictured my life differently than it is now." It's easy to blame Owen, but his choices didn't affect mine. I could have been working at a large firm and building a career. Owen may have gotten us further into debt due to his gambling, but I also would be making more money and therefore, able to pay the debts off faster.

Dani slams her hands on the table. "That's it. You're doing this, Holly. You're getting out of that hellhole and following your dream. Now, if you'll excuse me, I'll be in the ladies' room. You really shouldn't have let me have those fries."

She races away from the table before I have a chance to respond. Dani's right. I should pursue something with my degree. Could it really happen? Could I stop putting on my stupid polo and khakis daily and trade them for business attire and an office building?

Maybe. But I can't be too afraid to find out.

9

December doesn't start until tomorrow, but Mother Nature didn't waste any time. I wake the following morning to six fresh inches of snow—our first snowfall of the season. I take a few minutes to wake up more, rubbing my eyes and stretching my legs. I look out the window, and our street has been plowed. That's awesome because this street is often one of the last. Although it's a tad disappointing because I can't claim I was snowed in and still have to go to work.

Before I have my coffee, I pull on sweatpants, go downstairs and toss on my boots, jacket, hat, and gloves. My parents aren't up yet, and I want to shovel the driveway before they do. My dad will insist he does it, but I don't think that's a great idea. His hip surgery was last year, but better safe than sorry.

I open the garage door, grab the shovel, and start tossing snow aside. At least it's super fluffy, making it easier to move. Once I finish the first half of the driveway, I can quickly push a lot of it to the side and not have to lift as much.

The end of the driveway is what almost kills me. Once the

plow has come through, a fantastic mountain of packed, dirty snow is left at the end. Lifting this is like trying to pick up a boulder. I take a deep breath, the cold air against my cheeks, and sweat covers my armpits. Shoveling is a huge cardio workout.

It takes about twenty minutes to finish clearing the driveway. Before I return to the house, I stop and observe my work. There's nothing more satisfying than a shoveled driveway after the snow.

After I take my winter gear off, a piping hot cup of coffee is waiting for me at the table. My mom has also made me eggs, toast, and bacon.

"Thank you, Mom." I wrap my hands around the mug, and the warmth brings feeling back into my fingers.

"Thank you for taking care of the driveway. We should invest in a snowblower. It would make things so much easier." She sits across the table from me, a piece of bacon in her hands. She tears off a small piece and pops it into her mouth.

"You know, you've been saying that since I was a little girl. Dad will never let you get one. 'Put your muscle into it. It's a perfect workout.'" I mimic my dad's voice. "Once I move out, I may have to insist on it." I don't want them to have to shovel. My dad can't do it with his hip, and I don't want my mom to hurt herself.

"When will that be, honey?"

I stop with my fork hovering between my plate and my mouth. "I'm sorry?"

"Moving out. How is it going for you? Are you doing a good job paying down the debt? You know that Dad and I can help you if you need it. We can't pay it all, but we have some money we can give you."

Even though my mom always said I wasn't intruding, and she and my dad insisted I move in—rent-free—this isn't the impression she is giving me right now. "First of all, I'm not taking your hard-earned money to pay for my ex-husband's mistakes. Second, are you anxious to get rid of me or something?"

"Nothing like that." My mom finishes her bacon. "Look at you. You barely eat—"

"I'm eating now."

"Sure. Today. But many days, I see you grab a yogurt, and that's probably all for the rest of the day. I'm worried about you." She cocks her head at me like a Springer Spaniel. "Are you happy?"

"Yes, Mom. I'm happy. I have a job, you and Dad, and Viv. What more do I need?"

She reaches across the table and touches my hand. "Sweetheart, how are you feeling about Amy?"

"Amy?"

"Yes, Amy. I just... I can't believe Levi contacted you after all this time and brought up all these emotions."

"Mom, it's fine. It was kind of nice seeing him." I'm telling the truth. Levi is nice, pleasant to talk to, and not bad to look at, either. And seeing him is almost like a part of Amy has been brought back to me.

"That's fine, but I'm worried about what this will do to you."

I set my fork on my plate. "What it will *do* to me? What does that mean?"

"When Amy passed away, it took you months to get back to a place of normalcy. Your grades suffered, you snapped at Dad and me a lot, and you didn't want to attend any family gatherings."

"I was thirteen, and my best friend died. What did you expect?"

She pulls back, wincing. "See? This is how it was then. You don't normally talk back to me like that."

I push my chair out and pick up my plate. "That wasn't

me talking back. I'm an adult now, Mom, and I can handle this. Besides, it's not like I'll see Levi regularly or anything. He gave me the necklace, and that's it. There's nothing left for us to talk about."

"You and Levi? Or me and you?"

I put my plate in the sink. "Both."

10

My heart races as I desperately try to make it to work on time, despite the slippery roads post-snowfall. With my hands firmly gripping the wheel at the ten and two position and extra caution taken, I arrive only fifteen minutes late—a close call!

I'm shocked to see so many cars in the parking lot on what should be a quiet morning. I hastily park my car and quickly maneuver across the lot, the sliding doors opening in unison with my steps. My greeting to Bernice is a rushed wave as I nearly slip on the glossy floor. I grab onto a nearby shelf, pulling the merchandise to the ground.

Better the merchandise than me.

My cheeks flush in embarrassment as Bernice and Nora rush to my side to lend a hand. My body is rigid from the immense effort of holding myself upright, but thankfully I didn't take a tumble and hurt myself. From the ride here to this near-fall, it seems like I'm destined for an eventful day—for better or worse.

"Are you okay?" Nora asks. "What happened?"

"I'm fine." Sure, the floor is wet from people walking in

with their snow-covered shoes and boots, but this is practically a slip-and-slide. "Why is it so wet here?"

"I didn't realize this area was so wet," Bernice says. I'm grateful I'm the one who almost fell and not her. It could have been pretty bad if she had.

I look around the area and can't figure it out.

Then I feel it—the drops on my head.

"Shit. There's a leak." I usually wouldn't use curse words in front of Bernice, but I don't have the patience to be polite right now.

I call to Nora, "Can you grab a bucket and a 'Caution: Wet Floor' sign? It looks like Roofers Plus is going to be getting a call—I'm not surprised that this old flat roof has leaks. I need to hurry and get someone out here to fix it before it gets any worse."

When I call Roofers Plus, they state they can send someone out right away to survey the damage and give an estimate to fix it. We've worked with them for many years, and I know their pricing is fair. I know that no matter the cost, I'll be able to approve it.

"If you need me, I'll be in my office," I tell Nora, the floor supervisor. "Please let me know when the worker from Roofers Plus gets here."

Nora acknowledges me, and when I arrive at my tiny office, I fall into my chair and sigh. What a long day already, and it's barely after eight. I hope the rest of the day doesn't drag on.

I turn on my computer and open my scheduling app, dreading the headache I know I'm about to get. With restrictions, requests off, and certain employees that can't work together, it's always a challenge to create the perfect schedule. However, I always manage to find a way.

The gentle hum of my computer and the clock's ticking are the only sounds in the office as I frantically type away at the scheduling app. Suddenly, a knock on the door startles me, and I look up to find Nora in the doorway.

"Roofers Plus is here. The guy's up in front where the leak is. And by the way, he's yummy."

I raise my eyebrows. "Thanks. Yummy is the exact quality I need in roof repair, you know, besides competence." Nora doesn't come back with anything and exits the office. I head to the front to greet the roofing contractor.

As I approach the person standing in the front, the first thing I notice is how his jeans fit him snugly. With his back to me, I can't help but admire how the fabric hugs his backside. Adding to the cliché look, he's wearing a red and black flannel shirt.

"Excuse me?" I hesitantly ask, stepping a few feet away from him. When he turns around, our jaws drop in shock.

"Holly?"

"Levi. What are you doing here?" I say, already knowing the answer.

His smile is wide and inviting, and I can't help but notice the scruffy facial hair he's grown since the last time I saw him. He looks like a modern-day lumberjack, and I have to admit, I'm not mad about it.

"I work for Roofers Plus. I worked at their location in Riverview, and when I moved back here, they let me transfer. Wow! I knew you worked at a grocery store but didn't know which one. How are you?"

"The best I can since my store's roof is leaking."

"The young woman who greeted me said you almost fell, but took out the shelf instead."

Thanks, Nora.

"It didn't happen *quite* like that."

"Did you read the letter from Amy?"

He didn't wait to ask. I don't know if I'm prepared for this conversation. "Um, yeah. I did."

He tilts his head and purses his lips together, his expression of heartfelt curiosity and compassion evident. "Would you be able to tell me what it said? I know it's personal, and I understand if it's too much. It's just that it's an incredible gift, and it would be like I'm getting to hear from her, too."

Ouch. If he intended to punch me in the gut, he did, and with perfect aim. Having a letter from her, something that she wrote specifically for me, feels great. I'm sure the fact that he doesn't is hard for him. I can't tell him what she wrote about him, though. About the feelings he had for me.

"She told me that she loved me. That was pretty much it."

"Your cheeks are pink."

I touch my hand to my face. Sure enough, they're warm, too. Thinking about what she wrote in that letter makes me blush.

"I'm a little cold, that's all." There's no way I'm admitting what's inside the letter. I wonder if he remembers having a crush on me. That was so long ago. I'm sure he went through many crushes and relationships since then.

"Well, I better start working on this. I'll be outside for the time being." He pulls something out of his pocket and hands it to me. "Here's my work cell number. Text or call if you need me. I don't want you to come out in the cold if you don't need to."

"Oh, okay, thank you." I like he's making it so easy to reach him. "When you know the cost, please let me know. Find Nora if I'm not on the sales floor, and she'll page me."

"That sounds great. I'll get to work." He nods his head and walks away.

I find myself lingering as he steps out the door into the cold. I appreciate that he didn't press me about Amy's letter. It was easy to tell he wanted to know, though, and I feel like a jerk for not sharing with him.

Maybe another cup of coffee and talking about Amy isn't a bad idea.

AFTER A BRIEF SEARCH, LEVI FINALLY FINDS ME ASSISTING Bernice in the hair care aisle. We are both in awe of the decades-old stories she is sharing; from the momentous Apollo 11 mission to the iconic Woodstock festival, and how life has changed since then. Despite her enthusiasm for new tech, Bernice admits she struggles to use computers. I admire her greatly, and I can tell Levi feels the same way.

Levi hands me a sheet of paper with a quote for the roof repair. A quick glance reveals it to be a sensible price, so I agree since the roof must be fixed as soon as possible.

"Looks good. When can you start?"

"Are you sure you don't want to take the time to consider other quotes or speak to someone else about this job?"

"We always use Roofers Plus," I tell him, admitting I knew he had the job from the moment he arrived. "It's a stand-up company, and we have a relationship with them."

"I'm happy to hear that."

After glancing at Bernice, Levi places his hand on my arm and gently pulls me aside. His deep brown eyes hold mine as he speaks, his voice soft.

"I enjoyed catching up over coffee the other day. Would you be interested in getting together again?"

I want to talk with him more about Amy, retell some of our favorite stories, and maybe share the letter.

"Like a date?" My breath bottles in my chest as I await his response. Between Dani's remarks and Amy's letter, maybe that's what he wants.

He darts his eyes to the ceiling and back to me. "Um, no. Just to catch up some more."

Or maybe it isn't. Damn me for reading into it. Now he probably thinks I like him, and that's so far from the truth. We've reconnected after decades apart. I barely know him. Ugh. *This can't be happening!*

But it is. And I can't simply turn and run the other way. "Yeah. Sorry. I thought that was what you meant. I don't know why I said that. Let's hang out again. Coffee again?"

"I was thinking more like pizza."

"Pizza's good. I love pizza. Pizza's my favorite." *Shut up!* I sound like Buddy the Elf.

"Perfect. Pizza it is, then."

We stand there, nodding at each other in agreement. Where do we go from here?

Our moment is interrupted when the customer service desk pages me with a phone call.

"Okay, I'll text you the details. Can't wait," Levi says before turning and leaving the store.

As I anticipate spending more time with Levi, I'm overwhelmed with excitement. I can hardly wait.

I spend all day anxiously awaiting the moment I'll see my ex, Owen. I stand outside the door of my former apartment, my body tensing as I take in the not-so-safe surroundings. It's been a long time since I've been in this neighborhood, and although I always felt secure here with the familiarity of my neighbors, now I don't belong.

I pull my coat more snugly around me, feeling the bitter chill of the wintery day. Despite the temperature, I'm relieved it's not snowing; I'll take this cold over the snow any day. My gloved hand raps on the door, and I stuff my hands into my pockets as I wait for a response.

As I stand outside the door, it feels like an eternity until it finally swings open. With anticipation, I wonder if Owen has changed in the past few years. But instead of him, I'm met with a young woman with dark hair pulled back into a ponytail, eye makeup reminiscent of an 80's music video, a teal shirt with a ripped sleeve, and sweatpants with a hole in the knee.

"Whatever it is, we're not interested. I need to hang a 'No solicitors' sign on the door. Unless you're selling cookies or candy bars. Are you selling cookies or candy bars? I like mint cookies and caramel and chocolate bars."

I'm unsure what about me makes this lady think I'm here to sell her food. When was the last time she saw a Girl Scout? I'm a bit too old to pass for one.

"Hi. No, I'm not selling anything."

"Then what do you want?" She pulls her phone out and starts thumbing around. "I'm about to pass this level on Candy Crush."

Far be it from me to interrupt her swipes and crushes. I wonder if Owen moved. Our apartment didn't cost too much —only about six-hundred-fifty a month—but perhaps he couldn't swing it.

"Does Owen LaDolly live here?" I can't help but cringe when I say his last name. I *hated* that name. Holly LaDolly was my married name. What a joke!

The woman looks up from her phone, eyes narrowed. "Who's asking?"

I grit my teeth. I don't like this woman and don't even know her name.

"Holly."

"Holly who?"

"Owen's-ex-wife-Holly-who," I say firmly.

"Excuse me. What?" Her eyes are planted on mine like she is waiting for me to tell her I'm joking.

"Oh, he didn't tell you he used to be married?"

She shakes her head, waving her phone in the air. "No, no. I knew that." Her hot pink painted nails scratch her neck. "Well, he's not here right now."

My stomach drops. I mustered up all my courage to come, and Owen's not even here. I crane my neck and peek behind the woman. Clothes are scattered everywhere, and empty cups, takeaway containers, and plates overflow from the kitchen counter.

"Any idea when he'll be home?" I don't want to come back. I hoped to find the charm today and be out of Owen's life for good. So much for that.

"Late. He's at the casino."

Crap. He's still gambling. I had hoped he'd worked past his demons and stopped. Now I can't help but wonder if he's pushing this woman into debt, too. Is he gambling with her hard-earned money? And is she enabling him?

It doesn't matter. Not my problem.

"Okay. Can you tell him that I stopped by?"

She eyes me up and down, her judgments collecting on her face. Since she seems so straightforward and unable to hold her thoughts back, I brace myself for whatever she is going to say. Her opinions mean nothing to me, but I still don't want to stand here and be insulted.

"I really wish you had cookies," she says instead of hurling an insult at me. "Maybe I'll tell him." She shuts the door without another word.

I take a beat to gather myself before leaving. As I approach my car, I hear a door slam. I jump, take my keys, and shove my house key between my fingers should I need it.

I slowly look over and see that it's Owen.

While I recognize him, and it's only been a few short years since our divorce, he looks like he's aged about a decade. His once light blonde hair now has streaks of gray, the wrinkles in his face are prominent, and even though his eyes are still a piercing blue, he appears tired. So very tired.

We're silent for what feels like an eternity, the history of our relationship heavy in the air between us. I think of all the times we'd spent together—the dinners, the jokes, the fights. The tears and the anger. The bad moments had overshadowed the good ones.

"I didn't think I'd ever see you again." His voice is raspy, like he's smoked two packs daily for the past ten years. Maybe he has, and it's just another secret he's kept from me. I wouldn't be surprised. I've come to expect it.

"Hi." Back when I was talking to Little Miss Candy Crush, I had all the confidence in the world. Now, here I am with someone I used to love, and I can't even figure out what to say after the word hi.

It shouldn't be this complicated.

"What are you doing here?" He rubs his bare chin. He never could grow a beard, and he hated that.

"I met your girlfriend?" I phrase it as a question since I don't know for sure who the woman at the apartment is. She at least acted as she lived there.

"Oh, that's Sunny. She's a friend and is crashing with me for a few nights."

Sunny is quite an ironic name. I imagine her parents expected a cheery, optimistic girl and ended up with a dark, candy-matching rude daughter.

"She seems—"

"I know."

I'm glad it's not just me, then. "The reason I'm here." This is the most prolonged, drawn-out conversation I've ever had with him. When we first met, the words flowed easily between us. We were in sync. Eventually, our communication broke down, and I walked on eggshells around him. The shells still surround him, and I'm afraid to take that first step.

He steps forward, and I step back. I don't know what makes me do that.

"You can tell me."

The thing is, I know I can tell him. It's a matter of him cooperating and allowing me into the apartment to look for the charm.

I rub my hands together. "Okay. I'm sure I took mostly everything when I moved out, but recently I realized there is something I forgot."

"Sure. What is it? I'll grab it."

If only it were that easy. I wish I could tell him I left it on the counter next to the microwave, and I'd be done. It's more complicated than that.

Everything is always so complicated.

"The thing is, I don't know exactly where it is."

He rests his index finger against the bridge of his nose and turns it downward, past his mouth and chin. "Okay," he says softly. "What is it? I can look for it."

"It's a tiny charm. The kind that goes on a necklace."

The smirk on his lips and the glint in his eye make it clear he thinks I'm being silly. He never did understand the sentimentality of gifts, which was one of the many issues in our marriage.

"A charm? Next, you'll tell me it's for a leprechaun."

The old me would have rolled my eyes and stormed away, giving him the cold shoulder in protest. I bite my tongue and keep my expression neutral.

"Owen, please. I'm serious. It's something I had as a little girl. I've looked everywhere, and I can't find it. Chances are it's in the apartment."

He mulls it over, trying to decide between being a nice guy or a jerk. Which Owen will he be today?

"Well, it seems to me if this charm were *that* important to you, then you would have kept it in a safe place. Then you never would have lost it."

He will never understand, no matter how much I try to explain this to him. I never told him about Amy; even if I did, he probably wouldn't care. There's no way I can mention Levi. Next to his gambling addiction, Owen's jealousy often created a problem in our relationship. While we are no longer together, his learning about Levi will only worsen the situation.

"I don't want to argue, Owen. Can I please look around?"

He glimpses at the apartment building as though it holds the answer. The air is cold on my face, and I don't want to be here anymore. I need to either start looking for the charm or go home.

"I can't let you in tonight. Sunny would throw a fit. But I can have you come this weekend. Say, Saturday at one? Sunny has plans and won't be home."

Okay. Technically, I'm in. I may have to wait a bit, but at least I know it's happening. I actually got further than I expected.

"Okay," I agree. "That works for me. Thank you." Owen catches my arm as I turn to open my car door.

"Holly, you look great," he says.

I yank my arm away without acknowledging him.

12

L evi's apartment is a short five minutes from where he grew up on Ashbury Lane. I purposely avoid passing that street, not having been down it since Amy died. The thought of even seeing the name on a street sign almost sends me into an anxiety attack.

I pull into a parking spot and shut off the engine. I grab the Tupperware container that's still warm from the heat of the freshly baked chocolate chip cookies inside. The lid is slightly ajar, and I can smell the sweet aroma of sugar and melted chocolate. I hold it in my hands, feeling its warmth against my palms.

Levi buzzes me into the building, and when I reach his apartment, the door is already open. "Hello?" I call out, peeking my head in, unsure if I should enter without his explicit permission.

"You made it!" His beaming smile warms me. Levi reaches his arms out, and I go in for the hug, but his hands land on the container of cookies instead. My face falls, and I step back, embarrassed.

"You made cookies!" He pries open the lid, and a wave of nostalgia washes over me.

"Your favorite, remember? Whenever I came over, your mom always made chocolate chip cookies. We devoured them with a glass of cold milk."

I'll admit that Miss Candy Crush gave me the idea to bring cookies, since she thought I was a Girl Scout.

"Come in. Take your coat off."

I make my way to the galley-style kitchen that features a surprisingly small oven that I doubt could even fit a frozen pizza. The living room is straight ahead and has a plaid recliner that reminds me of my grandparent's furniture. The couch is an odd shade of green, but seems comfy enough. "I like your place." I shrug my jacket off, and he takes it from me.

"It's small, but it works." He sets the cookies on the counter and hangs my jacket on a hook next to the door. "The pizza should be here in about an hour. I ordered pepperoni and green peppers on it. I hope that's okay."

"Sure. That's fine." I hate pepperoni and green peppers. I'm a straight-cheese pizza kind of girl. I always have been and always will be. I don't want to be rude, so I'll push through and eat it.

He stares at me, his eyes narrowing. "Holly, nice try. I remember you're only about the cheese. That's what I ordered, heavy on the cheese."

"Wow," I say, genuinely impressed he recalls such a random piece of information from when we were kids. "Thank you."

"Would you like something to drink? A beer?"

"Sure." I lower myself onto the couch, my eyes scanning the room. They settle on a framed photograph of me, Levi, and Amy. The three of us are arm-in-arm, standing in front of a rustic log cabin.

"Camp Hummingbird. Remember?"

I press my hands against the cold beer can and I roll my eyes up at the ceiling to stop the tears. I can almost smell the campfire as I bask in the memory. "I sure do. That was one of the best summers I ever had. Canoeing, roasting marshmallows, and crafts."

"And sneaking out after the counselors went to bed."

"What? You did that?"

"You didn't?" He opts to sit in the recliner. He leans back and throws his ankle over his knee. "Every night that week, my buddies and I took off and hung out in the woods."

"Doing what?"

"Stupid shit," he mutters, a nostalgic smile on his lips. "Climbing trees, throwing rocks, howling to see if we could summon a wolf." He springs off the couch, ready to whoop and holler like any adolescent boy would in the forest. I shake my head, chuckling at the thought of him and his friends, their hands around their mouths to amplify their animalistic sounds.

"What?" he asks when he notices my laughter.

"Nothing. I'm just imagining it," I reply.

"You don't have to imagine it. I'm going to demonstrate."

His enthusiasm is infectious, but I politely decline his offer. "Maybe another time. I like the way it plays in my mind."

Levi shrugs and sits back down. "Suit yourself. How's work?"

There's a question. How much time does he have? "It's a job. I started as a checker in my teens and worked my way up to a manager. Sometimes it feels like all I do is push paper and put out fires all day. I enjoy interacting with most of the staff, but dealing with the owner's son is like walking through a landmine. He has no respect for me or anyone who works there. If I voice my issues with him to his mother, she'll fire me, not him. So, I am kind of... stuck."

Levi glances away from me, raising his palms toward apologetically. "Yikes. Why not do something else that you find interesting?"

I sink down onto the couch. "My degree is in graphic design, but it never went anywhere. I've accepted that this is my life. A polo and a khaki girl for life. Even corduroy at times."

"You do *not* wear cords. That's—"

"—kind of gross. That store is like the Arctic sometimes, though; as revolting as they are, they keep my legs warm." Levi arches an eyebrow at me, and I add, "Don't knock 'em until you've worn 'em."

"Noted. I'm curious, though, why didn't your degree take you anywhere?"

Graduating from college seems like ages ago. I adored my college years, and I had an absolute blast. Not only that, but I had such high aspirations for my future. What *did* happen?

"I guess I gave up. In my senior year, I interned at a marketing firm, and when they chose three of the five of us to stay on with them, I wasn't one of them. I still worked at the store part-time, so I moved to full-time. Life happened, and I got comfortable."

Levi runs his fingers through his thick, brown hair. "You have never had the opportunity to put your degree to use?"

"Nope. And now, so much has changed within graphic design. I'd probably need to take more classes to catch up. And I can't do that right now."

"Why not?"

Because I owe thousands of dollars in debt. People seem to have no problem flaunting money when they have it, but it feels shameful when you're broke, even if it's not your fault. "I'd have to live with my parents for the rest of my life to pay for classes! I'm out of there as soon as I have the money saved to do so."

Levi is quiet, and I tap on my beer can as I consider his thoughts. Is he judging me? Feeling sympathy? Or maybe I've just gone and made him super uncomfortable.

"Roofing, huh? How did you get into that?" If I move the conversation off me and my degree, then he won't judge *or* feel sympathy.

"Well," he takes another drink and then sets it on a corner table next to him. "College wasn't my thing. I didn't want to devote my time to earning a degree in something I didn't love. As a kid, I always enjoyed helping my dad build things. A friend offered me a few odd jobs at his company, and the next thing I knew, I had a full-blown career that I love."

"Climbing a ladder and standing on a roof with nothing to protect you? No, thank you. You're like a superhero in my eyes."

His laugh is infectious and hasn't changed since he was a kid. "A superhero? Like Spider-Man?"

I touch my finger to my chin as I think about all the superheroes. "Hm. No, I don't see you as a Peter Parker. A Robert Downey, Jr., maybe."

"Iron Man?" He nods in acceptance. "I'll take that. He's pretty much a legend."

"Maybe. If you're into tall, dark, handsome, and seriously sarcastic men."

He quirks an eyebrow, a mischievous glint in his eye. "Oh really? Is that so?"

My cheeks flush with embarrassment. I didn't realize my comment would make him think I was flirting. I meant it as a genuine compliment, but now I feel like I have crossed a line.

"Um... let's move on," I say awkwardly, my voice a little higher than usual. "Tell me about your dad, if you don't mind.

If it's too hard, I understand." I bite my lip, hoping I haven't made things even more uncomfortable.

"No, no. It's fine." He picks up his beer and grips his hands around it like a security blanket. "About six months ago, he had a stroke. He was transferred to a rehab center. Now he's moved back to a senior living facility."

"He's recovered then?" Levi's dad was always so nice. He often played games with us, took us to the movies, and threw the ball. I remember him as such a strong, independent man. It's hard to believe that he had a stroke.

"We'll see. Every day is different. As long as there aren't any setbacks, that's the hope. He's still so young, only in his late sixties."

My parents are still pretty spritely, save for my dad's hip. They are still very active, doing yard work and taking walks. My dad can't quite keep up like he used to, but he still has independence.

"It must be hard coming back."

"He wanted to. My mom and Amy are buried here. He wants to be close. In case." He shifts his eyes toward the ceiling. I want to sit next to him, take his hand, and let him find comfort in me. But I don't. I'm not sure if it's appropriate or not.

"So," he clears his throat. "Did you find the charm?"

"I wish I could say that I did. The good thing is, I think I know where it is."

"What's the bad thing?"

"It's at my ex-husband's apartment."

"Yikes. Are you comfortable asking him for it?"

"I'm already on it. I saw him yesterday, and he said I could come by Saturday and look for it. I'm sure it's somewhere in the apartment. I just need to figure out where." Based on the mess I saw when I peeked around Sunny, I don't anticipate this being easy to find.

His finger strokes the side of the can. "I'm sure you'll find it. These things always seem to have a way of working out."

He sounds like Sadie. I never considered myself an optimist, but on the other side of that, I never labeled myself as a pessimist either.

With that, the buzzer dings.

"Pizza's here. Your *cheese* pizza."

I start to stand to retrieve my purse. "Let me give you some money."

"No. It's one pizza. Besides, you bought my coffee the other day."

He doesn't give me a chance to reply, and he's out the door for the pizza. I stay in my seat for a moment, then figure I can help and get us some plates. There are only four cabinets in the small kitchen, so it doesn't take long to find them. I'm pulling them out of the cabinet when Levi comes back in.

"Oh my gosh, you got Ricardo's?"

"The one and only." He holds the pizza with one hand as though it's royalty. Heck, it kind of is. I haven't had Ricardo's in ages. The best slices around.

"I can't wait!"

He sets the pizza on the coffee table in front of the couch, and I hand him one of the plates. The garlic crust aroma strikes me when he opens the box. That's what Ricardo's is known for. Their garlic crust. It. Is. Amazing. I pull a piece out, the cheese dragging behind it like it's trying to catch up to the crust. I pull it off with my finger and wrap it onto the top of the piece.

I practically moan when I take the first bite. "So good."

Levi takes a bite, too. "I can't tell you how much I've missed this pizza." He sets his plate down. "You know, if we're eating pizza, there's something else we have to do."

"What's that?"

He grabs the remote and turns on Netflix. "*Back to the Future* marathon!"

A slight squeal escapes me. "Oh, yes! Pizza and Michael J. Fox. A perfect match!"

That was our tradition. If we had pizza at the Walsh house, we watched that movie. Nothing ever compared to the first one, but we watched all three.

I sat back on the couch and got comfortable, putting two more slices on my plate. If my mom could see me now. *Look, Mom. I'm eating!* I'm tempted to take a selfie and send it to her. Maybe then she'd leave me alone.

Yes, I'm more than annoyed at her nagging for me to eat. I understand why she does it, but that doesn't make it less annoying.

"You ready?" Levi asks.

I tell him yes as he presses the button to start the movie. I've never been more ready for anything.

13

I flutter my eyes open. I'm lying on a couch with a television in front of me. An arm is draped around me, and my head rests on someone's lap as a makeshift pillow. I internally groan as I realize the situation I'm in; I had fallen asleep last night while watching the third *Back to the Future* movie and slept on Levi's couch. With his arm around me.

I carefully slide out of his light hold. Once I escape the couch, I tiptoe to the door and pull my jacket off the hook. As I'm shrugging it on, I hear, "Good morning. Leaving so soon?"

"Oh, you're up. Sorry. I fell asleep during the movie."

I can't help but admire Levi when he sits up and runs his fingers through his hair. Little does he know, this small act of his entrances me. "Likely story," he says.

"What does that mean?" I zip my jacket.

"Do you remember when we watched movies, and you always fell asleep? That was a running joke in my house." I nod, recalling the countless films I've never seen the ending of. "Last night was fun," he continues, rubbing his hands on his thighs.

"Yeah, it was," I reply, thinking fondly of the conversations we'd shared about our lives, despite a few moments of sadness.

"We should do it again sometime. Maybe next time, go out somewhere."

Go out somewhere. That, for sure, sounds like he's suggesting a date. Is that where I want this to go?

"You look like a deer in headlights."

I stand there like I am, too. My heart is racing as I think of how I should respond. I'm flustered from waking up how I did, but maybe I'm reading too much into it—big deal. We fell asleep together. "I think that'd be great," I finally say.

"I'll text you or talk to you at the store."

The store! I pull my phone out of my purse. I have two missed calls and three texts from Nora. "I have to go. I'm late." I still have to stop at home, change into my work clothes, spray some dry shampoo on my hair, and brush my teeth. I'm going to be so late.

I yell goodbye to him as I race out the door, my phone in my hand. I hit the button to call the store. Customer service answers and I ask to be connected to Nora.

"Nora!" I yell into the phone when she answers. "I'm coming! I'm sorry I'm late. I'm going home to change, and then I'll be there."

"To change?"

"Long story. I'll be there soon."

As I hang up the phone, the soles of my feet slip on an unexpected patch of ice. My body slams into the hard ground in a split second, and my phone cracks against the cement. Tears fill my eyes as I slowly stand up, taking in the pain settling on my tailbone. When I reach my car, a bright yellow parking ticket sits underneath the windshield wiper—a reminder of the city ordinance that prohibits overnight parking on this street. I close my eyes and take in a deep breath as tears escape from the corners of my eyes.

Desperate for an escape from this sudden turn of events, an image of Michael J. Fox from *Back to the Future* pops into my head. If only I had a DeLorean at this very moment.

☙❧

I TIPTOE THROUGH THE FRONT DOOR AND AVOID detection by my parents. There's no time for a shower, so I brush my teeth and comb my hair before hurrying to work.

My heart drops like a rock when I see that my boss, Crystal Silver, has taken up residence in my chair. She sifts through the paperwork on my desk. A sly grin forms on her lips when she sees me.

"Miss James," she says, her tone dripping with sarcasm. "I'm glad you managed to find the time to come in today."

She presses her red lipstick-stained lips together and studies me with cat-like eyes. Her platinum hair reminds me of Meryl Streep in *The Devil Wears Prada*. Though compared to Mrs. Silver, Meryl's character was a gentle bunny.

"I'm sorry I'm late," I stammer, feeling cold air seep through my coat. "It's just... I overslept, and then slipped on the icy sidewalk, and... and then I got a parking ticket."

She raises an eyebrow, her stern gaze aimed directly at me. "That's quite the story. I hope, for your sake, it doesn't happen again."

The tension in the room is palpable as I move to the other side of the desk. My hands shake as I tuck myself into the chair.

"No, it won't happen again," I assure her. I don't want to be on the receiving end of her wrath.

"Good." Crystal grabs the paperwork off the desk, shuffles

it into a neat stack, and places it back down. Her fingers tap against the hard surface in an impatient rhythm.

"Now, let's get down to business," she says.

I stiffen in my chair, gripping the armrests. Business? I hadn't expected her to show up today and have no idea why she's here. "Okay," I reply, my voice cracking slightly.

Crystal nods. "First, great job handling the roof leak situation. I'm glad you went with Roofers Plus, as we always do. They expect to have it all fixed up in about a week. Well done."

I swallow the huge lump stuck in my throat. "Thank you." I can't help but think something not so nice comes after this compliment. Crystal isn't known for a complimentary demeanor.

"Praise belongs where deserved. And you deserve it." She wiggles her shoulders, crosses her hands, and intertwines her fingers. "Now, the reason I'm here. I want to talk to you about Scottie."

My heart, which had returned to my chest after tumbling onto the floor, now sinks again. She probably knows about the alcohol, but I'll end up being the one to deal with the consequences. She'll likely fire me, and Scottie won't have any repercussions.

"Yes, what about him? Is everything okay?" I ask, playing dumb. I don't know what Scottie may have told her, and I don't want to incriminate myself.

"He's fine. Wonderful, actually. He told me what a remarkable job you're doing as the manager." She gives me a warm smile, which slightly creeps me out since it's so unlike her.

I blink in surprise, utterly flabbergasted at the thought of Scottie having anything positive to say about me. "Thank you. I enjoy it."

"Good. I'm happy to hear you say that. Scottie does, too.

In fact, he likes his job so much he has aspirations like he's never had before."

This is new to me. Not once have I heard Scottie ever express interest in anything besides being a pain in the ass. The universe seems to be working against me, so I'll take this as a win.

"He's a fine employee." I stretch the truth farther than Mr. Fantastic's arms can reach with that one, but Scottie is her son, and offending Mrs. Silver isn't in my best interest.

I told Scottie as long as he paid back that money, which he did, I wouldn't say anything, so I'm not going back on my word now. That's not who I am.

"Fantastic. Scottie has expressed interest in moving out of the position he's currently in and transitioning to more of a management role."

"Excuse me? We're talking about Scottie Silver?"

"Yes. Why is that a surprise? You said yourself he's a great employee."

I know better than to correct her, but I didn't say great. I said *fine*. Those are on two different scales. I've dug myself a hole by not wanting to incriminate myself. "Sorry, you're right. He is. And that's great news that he wants to move up."

"Then it's settled." She claps her hands together. "Starting Monday, Scottie can start training as an assistant manager."

My head spins as I grapple with her words. She wants Scottie to be an assistant manager? He is clearly not suitable for the job. How can she even consider him for a position of authority? My stomach churns with anxiety because I know I have to accept this decision, even though I know it will lead to a disaster.

I'm going to regret this.

14

U nlucky for me, I'm the one offering Scottie the assistant manager position. I'd rather Crystal did it, but she said it would come across as nepotism if she did.

That's what it is, though.

Even though Crystal told me Scottie shows more ambition, she's not here daily. She doesn't see how her son acts and the disrespect he shows me. I hope he'll change once he's in a more prominent position. I can train him and pave the way for a decent working relationship. Perhaps, underneath it all, he's really a great guy.

Doubtful, I retch at the thought.

When Scottie knocks on my door, I want to crawl under my desk and pretend I'm not here. This situation is messed up. I can't blame anyone but myself for playing along. The second I found out Scottie stole from the store, I should have fired him. His mom might have understood.

No. That's not true. I've watched over the past year as she's treated her son as royalty instead of an employee. More than likely, she'd fire me for the mere suggestion of her son stealing. I can't afford that, not if I want to move into my own place within the next year.

"Come on in." I hold my breath as Scottie walks in, his khaki pants sagging off his hips and his polo shirt wrinkled and untucked. He's doused in cologne, a strong peppery scent mixed with tobacco. We'll have to work on his appearance.

He doesn't say anything as he sits across from me, his eyes wide and unblinking. His mother probably filled him in on the conversation we're about to have. I'm sure he's relishing the anticipation of my praising him. Squaring my shoulders, I prepare myself for what's coming.

This isn't my finest day.

"I hope everything is going well for you today." I dip my toes into the compliments with a pleasant greeting.

"I was on time, so yeah, it's good." He cocks his head as he delivers me a jab and hook. I wonder how many people know I was late this morning.

"Yes, you were on time."

"What's up, boss?"

How do you begin a conversation you don't want to have? I don't think Scottie is suitable for this job, but I don't have a choice. Everything is in Crystal's hands. What she says goes.

I groan inwardly and reach for the water bottle next to me. I wish it were alcohol, but unlike Scottie, I see an issue with working and drinking.

Scottie leans back in the chair and clasps his hands behind his head as though he's trying to appear authoritative. I hate that I'm about to give him some of that authority with this promotion.

"As you know, the store has been quite busy with the holidays. We're through Thanksgiving, but we still have Christmas to tend with," I start.

"Yes, after Thanksgiving comes Christmas. Then we have New Year's and Valentine's Day."

I force a smile and bite my tongue. "Yes, thank you for listing the holidays." I want to say something more snarky but instead, refocus. "Anyway, now is the perfect time to bring on an assistant manager. This person can help with scheduling, customer service, and day-to-day operations."

I hold my breath as Scottie yawns and nods. Crystal is the one pushing for him to get the promotion, but he seems disinterested, almost as if he is trying to avoid the responsibility that comes with it. "With all that said, I want to offer you the position if you're interested," I say.

He stares at me intently, his eyes boring into me with disdain for what reason? I have no idea. He remains silent, not giving me an answer.

I know he wants this job. Is he trying to intimidate me? "Is that a yes or no, or do you want to think about it?" I'm not a mind reader. If I were, I wouldn't be doing this. I'd be stupid rich and own an island somewhere, not succumbing to the unveiled threats of nepotism.

Scottie bites his lip and shifts his weight into the chair. "This is what *you* want, right? You honestly think I'm the one for the job?"

What is this kid doing to me? No, I *don't* think he's right for the job. Of all my employees, he's probably the worst of everyone that works here. I can't say that to him, though. I have to lie through my teeth in a way I never have.

I take a deep breath and force myself to take a different perspective—I'm here to help him. Maybe I can show him that he's worth more than the stolen goods he thinks will make him feel better. He's looking at me now like he's never had anyone believe in him.

I force a single word out of my mouth. "Yes." A chill runs down my spine, making me shudder. I look into Scottie's eyes and see a glimmer of relief. "If you want the job, it's yours."

"Before I accept, I want to say something."

I nod, my mouth slightly agape in anticipation.

"Thank you."

A puzzled expression comes over my face. "For what?" I ask.

"For not telling my mother about what happened the other day. You could have easily done that."

"Yes, I could have." I grapple every day with my decision to keep it to myself. It's nice to know he appreciates what I did, even if I think it might have been wrong for me to do so.

He crosses his arms and sulks down in the chair like a kid in study hall. "I know you didn't because you don't want to lose your job. I talked you up to my mom because of what you did, and then she suggested I become the assistant manager. I guess I will, then. So my answer is yes, but I assume you figured that before you even asked."

He stands up and pulls up his khakis, which inch right back down.

"If you're going to be an assistant manager, you need to get a pair of khakis that fit you."

"Right," he chuckles as he leaves the room with no other comment.

After the door shuts, I throw my hands in the air and silently scream. I could handle his sarcasm if I knew there wasn't some truth behind his words. He's not being sarcastic because he thinks it's funny. He's doing it because he knows how much it irritates me and that I won't—can't—fire him.

I slump down in my chair, sighing as I try to reconcile my feelings of helplessness with my desire to do my job well. I feel overwhelmed by the chaos surrounding me, from trying to pay off debt to searching for this charm. Scottie's presence adds an extra layer of complexity to the situation. I'm unsure how much longer I can juggle all these obligations and emotions.

What's worse is that I don't think I have a choice.

🜲 15 🜲

I lock myself in my office for a good portion of the day. Instead of calling an employee meeting, I email the staff informing them of Scottie's upcoming change in position. Phones are not supposed to be on during shifts, but I'm not stupid.

Midway through the morning, I have to check on Levi. He's been here most of the morning working on the roof repair. I haven't run into him once. As the manager, I should have greeted him when he first arrived.

Levi should be outside, but as I reach the front of the store, I spot him in the small café area. He's not alone. Scottie is with him, and they're both laughing.

I hate this.

Levi is a good guy, and I doubt Scottie will poison him with his unprofessionalism and a RadioShack-long receipt of annoying habits. On the contrary, Levi may be a positive influence on him. I just hate the thought of what lies Scottie may be spreading.

"Am I interrupting?" I ask, plastering on a fake smile for

Scottie, but I can't keep from beaming when my gaze meets Levi's.

"No, not at all." Levi swings a chair out. "Sit. I'm taking a break. The rest of the crew ate earlier. Scottie is keeping me company."

"How's it coming along?"

"Great. We should finish by the end of the week."

"That's why we love you guys." I feel my cheeks heat up as I realize what I've said, hastily correcting myself. "Well, the company, I mean. Roofers Plus does fabulous work."

"Miss James, Levi told me you two grew up together."

My stomach churns as Scottie asks questions, digging his nose where it doesn't belong. His presence is unwelcome, and I don't want him to know anything about my personal life.

"Yes, we did. Why don't you check the registers and make sure everything is running smoothly?"

"Is this my first official duty as an assistant manager?"

"If that makes you feel better, then yes."

Scottie salutes me like I'm a captain. He marches off, his shoes squeaking against the tile floor, and Levi and I remain at the table.

"Funny kid," Levi says, thumbing in Scottie's direction.

I shrug, picking at the napkins on the table in front of me. "If you say so," I reply.

Levi sets down his sandwich and leans forward on his elbows. "I sense some hostility. Not a fan?"

I sigh and shake my head. "He's been a bit problematic. I'd love to let him go, but his mom owns the store."

He nods in understanding. "So if you had your choice—"

"—he wouldn't be an assistant manager, a cart collector, or even an employee." When I offered him the position a few hours ago, Scottie fooled me into thinking he might be an okay choice. I know that's not the case, though.

Levi chuckles. "I'm looking forward to hanging out

again," he says, thankfully moving us away from discussing Scottie. The less I think about him, the better.

"Yeah, me too. What did you want to do? Go see a movie?"

"Nah. I'm not much of a fan of the movies these days. They don't make them like they used to."

I nod in agreement; many of my childhood memories are tied up with watching movies with Amy. We'd sleep over at her house, and her dad would make some homemade popcorn on the stovetop before we snuggled up in our sleeping bags on the living room floor to watch a movie. *Back to the Future* was one of those movies. I think back to the night before with Levi, waking up with him.

"We'll come up with something," Levi breaks me from my trance.

"My only request is nothing too cold, like ice skating."

Levi pretends like he's writing on an invisible notepad. "Nothing cold. Noted." He clicks his pretend pen and acts like he's sliding it into a chest pocket.

"I mean it, Levi."

"I know you do. Trust me. If there is anything I know about you is that when you're serious, you're *serious*."

He's not saying I'm a prude, is he? I like to have fun. Sure, I may not want to go bungee jumping or swallow swords, but I *know* how to have fun. However, with my dad in politics, I always had to be careful. Any misstep could mess up his career. Now that he's retired, I can relax. I don't want to go overboard, though.

"Anyway, moving on." I twirl a lock of my hair around my pointer finger. "Thanks for getting the roof repaired so quickly. That's why we use Roofers Plus so much."

"Fast, efficient, and quality work. That's us!"

A loud commotion near the entrance of the store breaks our conversation. Shouts and screams echo through the store as people scurry away in all directions. People glance around nervously, unsure of what to do.

"Watch out!" someone yells in my direction. I look up, and a pigeon is flying toward me, flapping its wings, clearly as freaked out as we are that it's inside the store. It's flying back and forth, like a ship trapped in a storm at sea.

All this poor bird wants is to find its way out. We're certainly not helping. The panicked pigeon flies past me. He narrowly misses the bread section before entering the dairy case with a whipping sound that echoes through the store. People continue maneuvering out of the pigeon's path like a giant game of dodgeball. Now he's back to where I'm standing and makes a beeline for Scottie.

"Someone, stand by the entrance and open the sliding door!"

Scottie races there before the pigeon reaches him. He stops and jumps on the pad to activate the sensor.

I put my hands over my head as the bird flaps toward the door. I hear a splattering of pigeon poop that lands directly on me. He's used me as his personal toilet.

The perfect metaphor for today.

S cottie's first real test as an assistant manager starts after the pigeon fiasco. He's on his own as I rush home to take the world's hottest and longest shower. I wash my hair three times and scrub my body so hard I'm surprised I'm not bleeding. Even after I'm clean, I still feel dirty. I don't think the feeling will ever leave me, especially with Levi having witnessed a bird defecating on me.

The rest of the day is mine as I take time off to regroup. I can't return to the store and face everyone—not yet—and I have errands to run, anyway. My parking ticket needs to be paid, and my phone screen needs to be fixed.

My phone is out of warranty, so I'm on my own to find a place to fix it. There is a small tech company on the way out of town that does screen repair. The building is run down with a stone parking lot, but they have fantastic reviews online. Plus, they're close, and I need my phone fixed.

Smartfix reminds me of a tiny cabin in the woods, a square building surrounded by trees, and a wooden ramp leading up to the door. The building has seen a slew of businesses, from auto repair to a bar, but Smartfix has been the longest-standing thus far.

The bells over the door jangle and announce my entrance, and the temperature immediately drops. I assume they keep the building cooler so the computers don't overheat. The smell of electricity and the dust from the vents fill the room. A man sits in a chair behind the counter, hunched over a laptop. He's bouncing his head to the music playing out of his phone.

"Be right there!" a woman calls out. The man doesn't even look up.

As I wait for assistance, I peruse the small store. They must do all their repair work in the back. The front area is reserved for selling items such as charging cables, phone cases, and pop sockets. I find a cute one with sloths on it. Maybe I'll buy it. I'll wait, though, since I won't have my phone for the time being.

"How can I help you?" I turn around to walk to the counter and stop. "Oh, it's you."

Sunny, Owen's friend, stands behind the counter with evident disappointment. It's like she expected diamonds and got cubic zirconia.

I'm not doing cartwheels over here, either.

"You work here?"

"What gave it away?" she replies. For the first time, I notice a nose ring. I want to rip it right out of her nose. This has nothing to do with Owen. I just don't like her.

"Anyway, my phone is cracked, and I need to have the screen replaced."

Sunny holds out her hand to take the phone, not offering pleasantries. Customer service is certainly not her forte, ironic since she's in the business, and the reviews often spoke of the kind staff.

"Wow. You really did a number on this, didn't you?"

"What gave it away?" I smirk at her, and she rolls her eyes. What? I can be snarky, too. Snarkier if I have the chance.

"Do you have a warranty?"

"Unfortunately, it expired."

She practically hisses. "Ouch. This will cost you then."

"Whatever it is, I'll pay." I don't have extra cash lying around, but I need my phone.

She sets the phone down and punches some things into a computer. "It'll be $227.37."

"Two hundred and twenty-seven dollars!" If I had been drinking something, I would have spit it out.

"And thirty-seven cents."

Ugh. This woman is sure a hag. If she can find any additional ways to irritate me, she does it. "I understand. Well, I need it fixed, so what can I do?"

"Next time, might I suggest not dropping your phone?"

Okay, that's it. Now the heat rises from my feet to my head. Even though this building must be thirty degrees, I could melt everything inside with how hot I am. I should ask to speak with her manager. Yes, I'll do that.

"Can I speak with your manager, please?" Just because she's not being polite doesn't mean I can't be. I can rise above her pettiness. I *will* rise above her pettiness, despite the thoughts I'm having.

"Owen!" she calls back behind her.

Wait, what? No. It can't be. Sure enough, Owen strolls in from the back, and when he sets his eyes on me, his eyes almost pop out of their sockets. "Holly."

"In the flesh." Here I thought it would be the long-haired guy hunching over the laptop, but he still sits where he was when I came in. I don't think he's budged. "*You're* the manager here?"

"Ah, yeah. I've been here about a year, and I've been the manager for about three months now."

I can't believe my luck today. It just keeps getting better and better. I might as well walk underneath a ladder and crack a mirror because I don't think I can do any more damage to my future at this rate. "So you two live *and* work together?"

Sunny folds a piece of gum and pops it into her mouth. "Yep. Do you have an issue with that?"

"Sunny, please." Owen puts his hand on her elbow, and she pulls away. "Can I have a second with Holly?"

Her lips pucker, and she looks at him for a few more seconds. She finally nods and walks into the back room.

"Wow. How did you manage this?" He picks up my phone and examines the damage.

I snatch it away from him. "I fell, and it broke my fall, okay? Any more questions?"

"Whoa." He holds his hands up. "What did I do?"

I sigh. "Nothing. I'm sorry. I'm just a little irritated with Little Miss Sunshine." I say that with the most sarcasm I possibly can. She's certainly not like the character from Mr. Men with pigtails, a sweet smile, and freckles.

He nods at me. "She goes through moods," he says, with an understanding in his voice. "She's not always like that."

"Somehow, I doubt that."

"You used to tell me not to make snap judgments."

"Well, people change. Anyway, I think I'll deal with my phone as it is. I'll be by Saturday to look for that charm." I turn and start toward the door.

"About that." Owen says, and my stomach lurches. Something isn't right. I can feel it. "Sunny would rather you didn't come by."

I whip around to face him. My gaze flicks between his eyes. "What?" The adrenaline pumps through my body, and my heart is now racing. "She tells you what to do, then?"

He presses his hand to his forehead, something he used to

do when he didn't know how to respond. Every time I asked him if he was gambling, he did that, and then a lie followed.

"Never mind." I don't even give him a chance to say anything. It's not worth making the situation worse by arguing with him when Sunny can hear us. "Then you find it for me. It's a charm about yay big," I gesture with my thumb and pointer finger to demonstrate. "It's a yellow boom box with a clip and a bell on it. Call me when you find it. You've got my number."

I pull open the door, the air rushing in behind it. It freezes my warm face for a second. I stomp back to my car, throw my broken phone on the seat next to me, and scream.

Worst. Day. Ever.

❧ 17 ❧

"**I** can't believe how big she is getting!" My palm circles Rose's back as I inhale her baby scent, and my uterus signals an alarm. Babies smell so amazing until they've filled their diapers. Still, I don't mind. I plan to have kids one day, whether with someone or on my own.

"She's growing so fast." Sadie pulls a blanket over herself and makes herself comfortable. "Thanks for coming over. Even if I don't sleep, it's a nice break. Dealing with a pep rally on the eve of a Full Moon is easier than some days with Rose, though I wouldn't trade my life with her for anything."

Sadie is the vice-principal of a local school, a job she has wanted for years. I'm so happy she has her dream job, and she's married to her high school crush, Joe, and they have this beautiful daughter.

"She's precious." Her big, brown eyes remind me of an animated baby. Bubbles push out of her mouth as she giggles.

"Okay," Sadie says as she pulls her knees up, the blanket still wrapped around her. "So Owen told you he won't let you come look for it? What a jerk!"

"I couldn't believe it either. He seemed so willing when I

89

first talked to him. Honestly, I have no faith whatsoever that he'll find it. The charm is so small, and from what I saw, the apartment doesn't look too tidy."

Sadie shakes her head. "This is Owen, too. He couldn't find his foot even though it's attached to his leg. Do you want Joey to go over there and put some wrestling moves on him?"

In high school, Sadie's husband wrestled for the school. He was outstanding, too, from what she tells me. "No. That won't solve anything. There has to be some way to convince him to let me over there."

Sadie raises an eyebrow.

"Um, no. Not even close to what I mean." I shiver at the thought of being intimate with Owen.

"Well, I don't know. I thought I'd mention it. How are you going to get in there, then? It sounds like this Sunny girl is nothing but clouds."

I laugh. "Not *even* clouds. She's more like a violent storm, a hurricane. There has to be some way I can appeal to him that this *woman* won't stand in his way. He hasn't said they're together, but I get the impression they are and she wears the pants in that apartment."

"Oh! Like Apartment Pants!"

"What?"

"It's an episode of *Friends* that Reese Witherspoon guest starred on. She went shopping and bought pants and called them Apartment Pants." Sadie laughs.

"You watch too much TV," I say.

"I watch the appropriate amount of television. I just so happen to watch the same show all the time."

"Maybe your extensive knowledge of television will come in handy trying to think of some way for me to get this charm." The last thing I want is to beg my ex to allow into his home. "I can't think of anything to convince him short of offering him money, and I don't have any of that."

"Holly!"

"What? I don't."

Sadie pulls her blanket tighter, covering her hands with it. "I know, but even if you did, you shouldn't give him money."

Rose wriggles in my arms and rubs her cute little face in the nook of my neck. She settles and puts her thumb in her mouth. "I know. I'm at a loss over what to do."

"Short of breaking into the apartment, I'm not sure what you *can* do other than hope and pray he steps up and finds it."

Breaking into his apartment is something I haven't considered. I still have a key, and he's probably not smart enough to have changed the locks when I moved out. Technically, I'm not breaking and entering if I have a key.

Sadie's hands reappear from under the blanket, and she slaps them on her knees. "You aren't seriously considering this, are you?"

"No, never."

"Yeah, that's why you've been silent for the last minute. You're trying to think of how to get away with it, aren't you?"

She slants her head, staring at me as she tries to read my thoughts. Disappointment is in the lines around her mouth and the set of her shoulders. I'm not the type of person to break into someone's home. I know that. She knows that. Do I have another choice, though?

"No. I'm not that dumb. I'll talk to him again when Sunny isn't around. She's probably about ninety percent of the problem. He was fine with my coming by until she voiced her opinion."

Once again, Rose begins to wiggle around. She lets out a piercing, smelly fart, and Sadie and I look at each other.

Sadie laughs hysterically, which startles Rose. "You should see the horror on your face!" She flips the blanket off and stands. "I think that was much more than gas."

"So take her." Rose lets out a whiny, short cry followed by

a longer one. I hold her out like she's a bomb ready to explode, which she very well might be.

Still laughing, Sadie takes her daughter from me. "Well, thanks for holding onto her that long, anyway. Sorry if you've lost your sense of smell."

As much as my eyes are watering from both the laughter and the smell, I can't wait until I'm the one changing diapers.

18

Through a series of texts, Levi and I planned a Saturday get together. He picks me up, and I avoid him coming into the house. I don't want my mom asking him a ton of questions like we're in high school, and this is a date.

Levi never said where he planned on us going, only that he'd pick me up around two in the afternoon. He hops on the expressway and drives south. I can't wait any longer on what feels like hour three of our drive.

"We've been driving forever," I say. "Are you sure this is the right way?"

"Have a little faith, Holly. We're almost there."

I cross my arms and look out the window. Despite the cold, it's a nice day; I guess it wouldn't be so bad if we got lost.

He smiles, reaching over and gently placing his right hand on my knee. "It will be worth it. I promise."

His hand on my knee sends a bolt of electricity through me. I try not to react, desperately hoping he doesn't notice

I'm blushing. I can feel my cheeks burning beneath a thin veneer of makeup, and I hope he doesn't notice.

It's not long before we exit the expressway. We drive past open, snow-covered fields. As we pass a few homes, I notice a snowman with branches for arms but no face. I can't help but think about when I had snowball fights with Amy and Levi. I can't recall the last time I rolled snow into a snowball.

"You better not be taking me ice skating or something. I already told you I'm not interested in anything that will be cold."

"What?" His eyes widen in a feigned mishap. "You did?" He glances off the road for a second, then back to the road.

Ugh! I swear, if he pulls up to an ice skating rink, I will be so mad. My butt is finally starting to heal after my fall the other day, and I don't want to take another tumble and potentially break something this time.

My arms are crossed in objection, though I smile the entire time. Even though he won't tell me his plans, I'm not mad. He's cute. And he knows it. His arrogant smile gives me butterflies, and I try to push them down and control them.

"Here we are." Levi turns his truck into a long, narrow drive. There is no sign indicating where we are, but it's a popular place as there are many parked vehicles. He finds a spot. "Make sure your gloves, hat and scarf are on. I'm not going to lie; this will be pretty cold."

"How cold?"

"Freezing."

"Is it too late to take me home so I can wrap myself in blankets and watch the Hallmark channel all day?"

"Come on. It'll be fun. I promise."

Though I haven't spent time with Levi in many, many years, there's one thing I do know; I trust him.

My boots hit the snow with a crunch. The vehicles have packed down the snow, which should at least make walking easier wherever we're going. We walk toward a large tent. Inside, a few tables are placed throughout, some providing hot chocolate and coffee, others presenting merchandise. A pathway riddled with snow and ice is visible just beyond the tent. A sign leaning against a pole near the tent entrance reads: "Welcome to the Winter Wonderland. The gift shop is just through here."

"Where are we?" I assume whatever we're doing is beyond the pathway.

"The ice caves."

"I've heard of these. I considered coming in the past, but by the time I thought of going, winter had passed."

"It's a good thing I brought you then." Levi reaches his gloved hand out, palm upright. Does he want me to hold his hand?

"I thought this wasn't a date."

He looks at me, and my heart kicks into a gallop. "It can be if you want it to be," he says.

Amy's note flashes in my mind. *Levi has always had a thing for you.* It's been over twenty years. He can't still have feelings for me, can he?

And even further, can *I* have feelings for *him*?

"Okay." I intertwine our fingers together. "A date it is." Suddenly I feel as though I've made some significant declaration by saying this.

We make our way through the tent and start on the path to the ice caves. The aroma of the coffee drifts away, and the crisp air is almost void of the chattering guests now. The walkway is serene, and I notice lanterns hanging on decorative metal poles that light the pathway in the evenings. I'm sure it's beautiful in the evenings.

"What made you decide to bring me here, especially knowing how adamant I was about doing *anything* outside? You're literally bringing me into an enormous ice cube."

Levi tightens his fingers with mine. "Do you remember when we used to make those forts in the winter?"

The memory warms me, still vivid in my mind. I can see Amy's face and remember how she used to laugh with delight when we built them. "Yeah. We'd pack up the snow and make it almost like a little house, and over a few days, it'd freeze. We'd hide out in there. I remember Viv trying to get me home for dinner, and we'd all be huddling in there until your mom came out and yelled at us."

He chuckles. "Ah, those are the best memories."

"They are." I love that they will live within me forever.

"I wish Amy were alive to see these. She would have been in awe of them. I thought we could come together and experience them in her honor."

Wow. After this reasoning, it's hard to be bothered by the cold. I feel terrible about the hard time I gave him earlier.

"I think that's a perfect idea."

The cold doesn't matter anymore. It's no longer biting at my face and making my cheeks numb. My body is warmed by the memory of my best friend, the good times we had together, and that I'm sharing this experience with Levi.

I'm not prepared for the enormity of the first cave as we approach it. It's towering, with icicles so large it's as though a waterfall is frozen over it. We step inside, and the inside is lit only by the daylight peeking in through the cracks and holes in the ice above us. The light reflects off the ice and snow within the cave. I'm in awe at the colors I'm seeing; pale blue tones with tints of white and some patches of deep blue-green ice.

"Is this safe?" I'm standing inside of literally tons of ice. What if a crack forms, causing ice to topple over us?

He lets go of my hand and puts his arm around me. "One hundred percent safe. They wouldn't allow us here if it wasn't. It has to be a certain temperature outside for this to be viewed. The park service monitors it and only opens it when it's safe."

"This is breathtaking. Our forts have nothing on this. Look at this." I rush over to a rounded piece of ice that looks like crystal. "Amy would have been speechless."

"Speechless? I don't know about that." At the memory of his sister, he smiles. "She always had something to say."

She did. She could never be quiet. I can picture her at the school cafeteria table, never finishing her lunch because she chatted through most of it. If I focus enough, I can even hear her voice.

"I miss her."

Levi comes up behind me and places his hand on my shoulder, giving it a little squeeze. "Me, too." He slides his hand down to the middle of my back, and I shiver. "Holly, can I say something?"

"Sure." I turn, and his breath is warm against my face. Our eyes are locked as we stare at each other, and his pupils are large, dark discs. His gaze is electric.

"There's something about you. There always has been. When we left town, I was so mad at my parents. I didn't understand why they wouldn't let me call you. They wanted to put everything behind them since we moved to a new town and no one knew about Amy. I'm so sorry."

"It's okay, Levi. We were teenagers. At first, I struggled with it. Eventually, though, I moved on and accepted I'd never see you again."

Levi shakes his head. "I didn't want to let that happen. Yes, for a long time, I pushed it to the back of my mind—all of it—but when I found that necklace and the letter, I took it as a sign."

Signs again. Everyone in my life seems to be obsessed with them in one way or another. It's not that I *don't* believe in them. I don't know what I think about them. What he's saying, though, makes me think that perhaps everything in Amy's letter is true. Levi did have feelings for me at one time and maybe he still does.

If I kiss him, will he respond? We've never been this close before, and I'm not sure how he's feeling. Maybe I'm reading too much into his words, and he doesn't intend anything by them. On the other hand, perhaps he wants to kiss me. What do I do if he tries?

"I think it's a sign, too," I blurt out, preparing for the kiss I'm sure is coming. My eyes flutter shut. I uncross my arms and curl my fingers around his hand. My eyes flash open when he pulls his hand away and steps backward.

"I'm so glad you responded to me, and we're friends again."

Friends.

I'm such a fool.

"Yeah, me, too. It's nice to have friends." It's nice to have friends? What a weird thing to say. But that's me lately. Weird to the core. I can't read any situation correctly. I read him wrong, I read Scottie wrong, I read Owen wrong. What's next?

"Should we move on to the next cave?"

A cold, bitter wind whips through the cave as I nod. I want to escape this, but I oblige and make small talk as we complete our day together. I don't understand. He told me that if I wanted this to be a date, it could be a date. So why reject me when a kiss was inevitable?

Later in the afternoon, Levi drops me off at home. The back door shuts behind me, sealing in the warmth. He drives off as I stand in the living room, alone. I'm happy both my parents are gone, and I don't have to face them as I hold back tears. They'll question what happened, and I can't respond if I don't even know the answer.

19

I arrive at work the next morning ready to take on the day. I've already had two cups of coffee, and I'm not feeling that perky yet, so three should do the trick. My heart is beating wildly, and I feel like a racehorse being released from the gate. My cheeks are tingly, my hands are darting, and my mind is racing a million miles an hour. I probably seem manic to everyone around me, but I don't care. I need to move past yesterday's awkwardness and pretend it never happened.

Dani called in the evening, hoping for me to detail my time with Levi. I didn't divulge too much, only telling her I had fun. Considering she didn't ask if he kissed me, I think she sensed the day wasn't perfect.

I dart through the main aisle back to my office, forcing a smile to my face. It's funny how even if you don't feel like smiling, once you do, your attitude can change. Even before pouring that third cup of coffee, I'm perking up.

"Wow! Why are you so happy?" Scottie asks as I walk into my office, which has now become *our* office. I used to be able to get away from him in here. Now I have to hide in the bathroom if I want some space.

I pause as I consider the question. "I don't know. I'm alive and healthy. Isn't that something to be happy about?"

"Sure. But not this happy. This level of smiling should be illegal."

"No. Do you know what *is* illegal? Stealing wine." I bite back at him before I have a chance to stop myself. "Sorry." I pull my jacket off and hang it on the hook, my smile wiped clean off my face. "That was out of line. How have things been this morning? Any issues?"

"Pretty good. Bernice left about an hour ago. She wasn't feeling well and had a fever."

"Oh no. I hope she's okay."

"She said she'd call you tomorrow and let you know how she's feeling. Meanwhile, I called Justine in, and she's covering the shift."

I'm impressed that Scottie even thought to call Justine. She's a very part-time employee that we refer to as a floater. She comes in whenever we need her, pending she's available. She only works odd jobs, and it comes in handy. I can only think of one time she wasn't available when we needed her.

Today he's proven himself. I'll take it and only hope it continues. And I'll need the win to maintain this fake happy mood.

"What are you doing in here?" I ask. "One of us should be on the floor." The picture on my desk of me with Dani, Viv, and Sadie is off center. I shift it back to where it should be.

"Sorry. I just got off a call with my mom. She wanted to check-in. I told her that things couldn't be better." He gives a crooked smile, taunting me.

I clench my teeth, forcing a smile onto my face. I don't trust him. I didn't before he stole the wine and I can't now. He isn't forgiven just because he paid the store back. He could be trying to get on my good side, but I'm not so sure about that. Not telling Crystal was stupid.

The dumbest thing I've ever done. Well, next to thinking Levi wanted to kiss me.

Scottie leaves the room, and before I even sit down, Nora pages me over the loudspeaker. I'm needed at the customer service desk. Great. I thought I could forcefully be cheerful, but after that minor run-in with Scottie, I'm not sure.

Hopefully, I'm not dealing with an angry customer. That's the worst part of this job, I think. People have screamed at me because an apple in a bag had a bruise or ice cream had melted. Yes, on a ninety-degree day, someone returned to the store irked that it melted on their way home. Some people have no common sense.

My employees put so much work into making sure the store is clean, functional, and that we help in any way that we can. The shelves are always stocked, and it's never impossible to find help on the sales floor, like in some other stores.

This is the job I've signed on for, and I take it seriously. I'm a strong woman, and I can handle whatever awaits me. I slap my hands down on my desk, stand, stretch out my arms, and go to the customer service desk.

Levi is waiting for me there. He's holding a sheet of paper in his left hand, and his right arm rests on the counter.

"Holly, good morning."

"Hey, Levi. Why didn't you come back to my office? You didn't have to have me paged."

He hands the paper to me. "Here's the bill." He says the words in a monotone voice that sounds detached.

"You finished already?"

"Yeah. My guys started early this morning so we could get it done for you. They're calling for another big storm this weekend. The store should be protected."

"Well, thank you so much. That's wonderful."

It isn't lost on me that he isn't making eye contact. Our communication is entirely transactional. This isn't how friends act toward one another. Is this because of what happened yesterday?

"So, big plans this weekend?" I ask him this, trying to start some conversation.

"Not really. With the storm coming, I'll probably hunker down. Maybe watch a few movies."

Movies. I can't stop thinking about the night we shared on his couch and shoved popcorn in our faces. Did he want to do it again?

"Do you want to watch together?"

"No thanks. I have plans."

My heart sinks in my chest. Did he reject me? He didn't give it much thought before answering. I chew my bottom lip as I consider asking if his plans are with friends or a woman.

"Oh. Okay."

He grins and gives me a friendly bump on my shoulder. "Maybe another time."

Even though he says the words, he doesn't sound convincing. There is something in the way that he turns his body, a stiffness in his shoulders, a tension in his eyes, that tells me this isn't what he wants.

I don't know what to say. "Thanks for fixing the roof. We'll get this paid right away."

"Great. Thanks." Levi walks past me, leaving me standing at the counter in disbelief.

Scottie pops up like a fly ball at a ball game. "That dude just turned you down like the volume on a stereo! You must be so embarrassed."

I wave my hand at him and rush away to the bathroom. I need to compose myself before I burst into tears.

I squirm around in the front seat and pull a ski mask over my face. I wriggle out of my coat, remove a pair of black leather gloves from my pocket, and slip them on. This is stupid. This is really, really stupid.

Yet I'm doing it.

Dani shifts the Volvo into park and looks at me straight-faced. "Let's go."

She opens her door and waits for me to exit the car. The cold night air slaps me in my eyes when I open my door. I snatch my jacket off the back of the seat, slip it back on, and follow Dani across the street up to Owen's apartment building entrance.

I stare at the apartment complex. I could be at home eating ice cream, but I'm here to do something unimaginable. Should I turn right back around now? I could say a bad idea is better than no idea, but Dani's right. This is my decision. I can back out if I want to, but the charm will be stuck here forever.

"What are we doing?" I ask her, desperate to conjure strength from her confidence.

"We're here for the charm, and that's all we need to be doing. Now let's go or go home."

I let out a breath as I realize all it takes is a turn of the key in the lock and some creative searching, and the charm is back where it belongs. With me.

"Okay. Let's do it."

"Out of the way!" Dani whispers as she pulls me behind a tree. She points at two figures crossing the street. Owen and Sunny are on their way to the parking lot. "My gosh, if we'd stayed in my car any longer, they could have seen us. I thought they were gone already."

"They were supposed to be. They must have been running late." Dani convinced her college-aged daughter, Neveah, to go to Smartfix, chat it up with Sunny, and invite her to a party a friend was having. "They're leaving now, so at least we know we have a lot of time."

We patiently wait for Sunny and Owen to get into his car. It's dented and rusty, with a ragged line of rust down the side and one of the hubcaps missing. It squeals out of the space, leaving us in the clear.

"Okay, Holly, are you ready for this?"

"No," I say honestly, my heart racing. I am already sweating through my shirt underneath my jacket. "What if we get caught?"

"We won't get caught. Besides, we have a key. It's not like we're picking a lock or something. That would come off as suspicious."

"And two people in all black and ski masks don't?"

"It's cold. No one will think twice about it. Now, let's go."

The faster we are in and out, the better. I take a deep breath and mutter a silent prayer before turning the key. The door cracks open, and Dani shoves me inside. I almost trip over the arm of the couch but catch myself in time. The door squeaks when she shuts it behind me.

"I heard someone talking in the next apartment." She glances at the clock on the wall. "Let's get this done."

I push aside my racing thoughts and survey the living room: a brown, ripped leather couch with a partially crumpled throw blanket; an end table with textbooks piled onto it; a coffee table with a lamp next to it.

I look up at Dani, who is wearing a faded denim jacket zipped up. "Can we get started, or are you taking inventory of the room first?"

I nod and motion for her to follow me to what appears to be the bedroom. The room smells stale, and the bed has messy sheets and pillows thrown about. A nightstand sits next to the bed with a lamp on it, books stacked haphazardly around it.

"Actually, maybe we should split up. You start in the kitchen. Check all drawers and cabinets. Remember, it's pretty small, maybe an inch, yellow. Keep your eyes open."

"Got it. Small, yellow, eyes open. Neveah is texting when Owen and Sunny leave the party, so I'll let you know if I get anything."

Once Dani is out of the room, I check the nightstand. I actually bought this piece of furniture right after our wedding. It was on my side of the bed. When I moved out, I decided to leave it behind.

It's weird seeing it here, knowing the items I used to keep inside. I slide open the drawer slowly, like it's a jack-in-the-box. Who knows what I'll find in there now?

At first glance, nothing surprising jumps out at me. An old watch lays in the corner, the one I think his sister bought him for Christmas one year. A few birthday cards are next to the watch, along with some cough drops and a few charging cords. I take everything out and carefully place them on the bed to access the back more easily. I reach my hand back and pull out a box of condoms.

Gross.

I mean, I'm glad he's using condoms. I just don't want to picture him and Sunny. And, of course, that is all I can do now.

The rest of what I find is of little to no worth. Tiny knick knacks like those you'd find in a claw machine. What is he doing with all of this? I don't find the charm, and I carefully put everything back in place so he doesn't know anything has been moved.

I spin around the room. The dresser is the next thing I can tackle.

Sifting through the dresser, I see crisp shirts neatly folded and arranged in the top drawer. I wonder how he affords many of these high-brand shirts.

The smell of cedar wafts up as I open the next drawer. It's filled with an assortment of socks and leather belts. There is a lot of open space, and I can easily see what I'm looking for isn't there.

The bottom of the dresser is full of women's clothing. Wild-colored panties, skimpy tops with sequins, and sheer bras that appear worn out. I think I've established now that Sunny lives with Owen. I don't want to see her underwear. I shove the drawer closed.

The only place left to check is the closet. It's small, and when I open it, it's packed to the brim. A few long-sleeved shirts hang, clattering slightly against the door. A shelf on top that seems to have random items thrown about. The floor is non-existent, with clothes, small boxes, old shampoo bottles, and even a guitar with broken strings. How can I even start scavenging through this? I have to pull each item out one by one, and I'm sure that will take much too long. They will be back before I finish.

Frustrated, I shut the door and return to the kitchen to check on Dani. She's sitting on the couch, squeezed into the one spot with any space, watching *The Tonight Show Starring Jimmy Fallon.*

"What are you doing? I thought we were searching for the charm."

I angrily turn off the television.

"Sue me. I took a break. My back started hurting, so I sat down for a second. Any luck?"

"What do you think?"

"I don't know, which is why I'm asking you."

Laughter outside the door startles me. I race to the door and look out the peephole.

"They're back!" I whisper to Dani. "I thought Neveah was going to text you when they left."

Dani sticks her hand in her jacket pocket. "Shit! I left my phone in the car."

"You left it in the car!"

"That's what I said. We don't have time to argue. We have to go out the back window."

"We're on the second floor!" I don't have a death wish, or at the very least, I don't want to break my legs.

Dani takes my hand and leads me to the back of the apartment.

"You don't even know where we're going!"

"Shh." She slides into the bathroom, pulls me into the shower, and shuts the curtain.

"What are we—"

She puts her fingers to her lips as the door to the apartment opens. Owen and Sunny enter, still in the throes of laughter. Dani and I hold hands tightly as we listen to the two of them.

"I'll be right in, Sun. I have to take a leak," Owen says as Sunny replies in a seductive tone, "I'll be waiting."

Owen doesn't bother shutting the bathroom door. We both cringe as he lifts the toilet seat. The sound of rushing water fills the air. He lets out a long sigh before flushing. He leaves the bathroom without washing his hands. I press my lips together and hold back the urge to gag. We endure in silence until we hear him slam the bedroom door shut.

We pull back the curtain and tiptoe our way to the front door. Once outside, we race down the steps to the car. Dani's phone is on her seat. Four missed texts from Neveah and two calls. Had Dani had her phone, everything would have been okay. I'll admit it was a bit of an adrenaline rush, though.

"I can't believe we did that!" I say to Dani. "I didn't find anything, though, which sucks. I don't know what to do now."

"You'll figure it out. If I have to break into his apartment fifteen times, we will get that charm. I promise."

The thing is, I know she's being serious.

21

After work, I meander through the drive-through at a fast-food restaurant. I order a burger and fries, and while they are not the healthiest choice, I am not in the mood to cook, and my stomach is rumbling. Over a milkshake, I struggle with whether to call Levi or not. I don't feel capable of talking to him about what happened, but I'm wound up tight and need to vent. I wonder if I'll see Levi again or not.

Screw it. My mind won't let this go unless I face him and find out myself. I crumple up my burger bag, open the top of my now-empty milkshake, and shove the bag inside.

I pull up in front of Levi's apartment building a few minutes later. I sit in my car for a couple of minutes, letting the cold seep into me and numb the anxiety from the pit of my stomach. I gulp some air, straighten up as much as possible, exit the car, and head into his building.

I press my ear to his door. TLC's "Waterfalls" plays in the background, muffled. I remember how much I used to love that song. I knock, and the music cuts off. I hear Levi shuffling about inside.

"Levi? Are you there? It's me, Holly."

"Yeah." His voice cracks. "Hold on."

The door opens, and Levi stands behind it. His eyes are puffy and red, like he's been crying. He sniffles.

"Um, did I catch you at a bad time?"

He shakes his head. "It's fine. What's up?"

My pulse quickens as I realize I have nothing prepared, and he certainly doesn't seem like he wants me there. He opened the door. At least, that's something.

"I contemplated even coming here. What happened at the store was awkward, and I can't stop thinking about it."

Levi shifts his weight as he leans against the door. "Sorry about that. I didn't mean to come off as cold."

I'm not sure how he could have thought he'd come off any other way. "I'll admit, our interaction didn't exactly give me the warm fuzzies."

Just like in the store, he gives me the cold shoulder. Should I even bother talking to him about this? I know if I don't, I'll drive myself crazy thinking about "what if?"

"Okay, I won't keep you." I inhale a deep breath, giving myself one last moment to back out. I'm brave, though. I can do this.

"I know I didn't share Amy's letter with you. That's because she said something in there. She told me you had a crush on me when we were kids."

I wait for him to react, but his face is as still as a statue.

"I didn't think too much about it, but the more time we spent together, the more I started developing feelings for you. This doesn't often happen, me feeling some connection with someone, but I feel it with you. I thought you did, too, and then this morning, when you rejected me—"

"Rejected you?" He tilts his head to the side. "All I said was today isn't a good day to hang out."

"I thought—"

"What? You thought I was saying I didn't want to see you again? That's not it at all. In fact," he says and then pauses.

"What?"

He steps forward, runs his hand across my cheek, and presses his lips against mine. His lips are soft, warm, and heavy, like a blanket in winter. Our tongues dance in a duet of fluttering beats and paces. When he pulls away, I draw in a deep breath, and my heartbeat thumps relentlessly in my ears.

"What does that tell you?" Levi asks.

"I'm more confused than ever." The kiss was amazing, but not at all on track with what happened earlier today.

"Do you want to come inside?"

I step into his apartment. Even though I've been here before, it feels different somehow. Sad, almost. Two empty beer bottles sit on the coffee table. The lights are dim, a blanket is bunched up on the couch, along with crumbled up tissues.

"Um, did I interrupt something?"

"It's fine. Let me clean this up." He takes a small trash can, puts the tissues in, washes his hands, folds the blanket, and asks me to take a seat.

I sit at the end of the couch, wondering what he will say to me. "Were you listening to TLC before?"

"Oh, yeah. I was."

"What exactly is going on here?"

Levi's eyes widen. "Oh no! You thought I was—I mean, you thought—no, no. Nothing like that. I was—how do I put this?"

He stares at the ceiling like it will have the answer he needs.

"Just put it." I press my hands onto either side of me, pushing them into the couch.

Levi stands a few feet from me, crossing his arms. He

looks so uncomfortable. I have a terrible time trying to read him.

"I'm sorry for the way I acted this morning. Today's a difficult day for me."

Levi looks away from me. A buzzing fills my ears as my mind struggles to put two and two together. Today is the anniversary of Amy's death. "I'm sorry, Levi. I'm a terrible person for not remembering."

The first anniversary was tough. I cried. My mom offered to take me to Amy's gravesite, but I couldn't go. Slowly, that one day a year became easier, and eventually I didn't think about it anymore. It dawns on me that I haven't remembered for well over twenty years.

Not until Levi came into my life, anyway.

What kind of person doesn't remember the day her best friend died? How could I forget when I think about her all the time, even if I don't pinpoint that one terrible day?

"Don't." He takes a knee next to me and takes my hand in his. "I know you loved her—*love* her. Trust me. Remembering what today represents isn't easy. I didn't have any plans tonight, Holly. I just knew I wasn't in any capacity to be entertaining tonight. I've been in and out of tears most of the evening. I turned on TLC because she loved listening to them."

I laugh as I think about Amy and me dancing around her room as we listen to the tape. "We were so young we didn't even understand the meaning behind half of those songs."

The muscles in my chest tighten, and I'm not sure how much longer I can keep my sobs at bay. Without hesitating, Levi burrows his head into my lap and releases the tears he has been holding back. I run my fingers through his hair and look at the ceiling as I try to think of comforting words.

"I miss her so much," Levi cries, his voice cracking.

"I know, Levi. I miss her, too. She was amazing, and she would have achieved incredible things."

He lifts his head. "It's just not fair. I wish it had been me instead."

"Don't talk like that, Levi. She didn't deserve it, and neither did you. Cancer is an asshole of a disease. It doesn't care who it hurts, it just takes people and destroys them, and there's nothing we can do about it."

Levi moves and sits next to me. "I went to her gravesite today and brought her flowers." His voice is thick with emotion.

I smile. "She was allergic."

"She would sneeze uncontrollably if she came within a few feet of a bouquet."

"Always at least five short ones."

Levi nods. "That's right. Well, now she can enjoy them at least." He pauses. "I told her that I'm in contact with you again. I think she'd be happy about that."

Amy would be in awe of her brother now, watching the man he's become. I pause for a moment, take his hand in both of mine, and smile. "I do, too."

"Did you find the charm?"

I shake my head. "No luck yet. I hope it's not lost forever. It doesn't help that my ex and his new girlfriend are freezing me out and not letting me search for it. I had to break into his apartment to look myself."

"You what?"

"My friend Dani and I used my old key and searched his apartment when he wasn't home. Then he came back while we were there, and we had to sneak out. He almost caught us."

Levi crosses his arms. "Well, I guess that's something I never expected from you. Since we were kids, you were always doing the right thing."

"Not to mention, my dad would kill me if I did anything wrong. Even though he's not in politics anymore, something tells me he would not be happy if he found out about this."

"I think I'd have to agree."

My eyes lock in on his, and every nerve in my body tingles as we stare at each other silently. The thought of kissing him repeatedly makes me giddy, even though we haven't moved our lips closer together yet.

He looks at me softly and brushes a lock of hair behind my ear. "Stay with me tonight, Holly."

My heart races as I smile and whisper, "I'd love to." My smile broadens. "Just let me move my car first."

The last thing I want is to wake up to another parking ticket.

22

When I wake, Levi is sitting up in bed, watching me. His eyelashes are long as he blinks at me. "Morning," he whispers.

"Morning." I reach my arms overhead for a big stretch. "I wish we could spend the day in bed."

Levi nods and kisses my hand before pulling me into his arms. Together, we sit and watch the sun begin to emerge through the shades.

Eventually, I have to leave for work. I stop by my house to shower and change clothes. Luckily the snowstorm wasn't as bad as predicted, and I didn't run into any issues on my way in.

The store is a flurry of activity, and I'm crisscrossing the sales floor, answering questions and keeping an eye on the registers, which are spitting out receipts steadily. The store is packed, and it's been this way since ten this morning. Every aisle is clogged with shoppers. Employees rush from display to display, collecting empty shopping carts left behind.

I order my lunch from the local sub shop and eat in the break room. I'm one of the first to have lunch today, so I eat quickly and return to work. I'm grinning the entire time while I eat, unable to keep Levi off my mind.

That's okay. I don't want to stop thinking about him.

As soon as I take my last bite, I'm paged through the loudspeaker. I pick up the closest phone and call Nora.

"Hi, Holly. There's someone here to see you."

"Okay." Sometimes I have potential vendors popping in or someone trying to sell me something they think the store may need. I want to put myself in the right space for whoever I am dealing with. "Did this person give a name?"

"He says his name is Owen."

A sinking feeling fills my belly when she says this. What is he doing here? "Please send him back to my office." I hang up the phone, and my chest constricts, a film of sweat breaking out across my forehead.

When I return to my office, Scottie is sitting at the desk, eating licorice.

"You're going to have to leave. I need the space."

"For what?" Scottie takes a bite of his licorice. "I'm eating my lunch."

"Licorice for lunch?"

"It's not licorice. They're Red Vines."

I roll my eyes. Same thing. "I don't care what it is. Get out." I point toward the door.

"Wow." Scottie stands and wraps his hands around his candy. "I'm not sure what your deal is, but I do *not* like this energy."

What is he even saying? My *energy*? Maybe he had a little of that wine today. I don't want to know.

"Excuse me?" Owen rattles a knock on the door.

He's wearing a huge, puffy blue jacket that reminds me of a blueberry. I hold back a laugh.

"Who's this?" Scottie asks, like it's any of his business.

"Don't worry about it. Come on in. Scottie—out." I point to the door again.

"See ya, man," he says to Owen like they're old friends. "And good luck."

Owen doesn't respond, which I am happy about because the last thing I want is for them to get involved in a conversation. Then I'd have Scottie asking me a hundred questions and making unnecessary comments.

"He seems—"

"—he's an idiot," I reply, interrupting him. I believe that now more than ever. Even though he is doing a fine job as assistant manager, it doesn't change the fact that I find him frustratingly annoying. "What brings you here?" I ask.

He reaches his hand out to me, palm up. When I look down, I see a single key shining like a jewel in the middle of his palm.

I didn't.

"I believe this is yours. I found it on my kitchen counter."

I stare at him impassively. "I don't know what that's for," I lie.

"Yes, you do. I wasn't aware you still had a key to the apartment. My neighbor said he saw two people go in almost as soon as I left with Sunny. Why were you in my apartment?"

I know how this looks, but I have to deny everything.

"I don't know what you're talking about."

"Come on, Hol. Don't do this."

I pause, unable to keep the irritation out of my voice. "I haven't been called Hol for years, and it was only ever by you. I hate it now."

Adrenaline surges through me and makes my hands shake as I take a deep breath and exhale. If I keep this up, I'll get myself in deeper trouble. "Fine," I say. "Fine. The other day I went in when you went to that party. I wanted to find my charm."

He rakes his hand through his hair. "I told you I would look for it. What gave you the right to come into my apartment and look through my things?"

He's upset and I understand why. I'd be angry, too, if he did the same to me. "I know, Owen. I'm sorry. I don't know what came over me. That charm means so much to me."

He wraps the key back in his palm and shoves it into the pocket of his humongous jacket. "I'm keeping this. Even though I shouldn't after what you did, I promise I will find that charm."

I don't believe him. Sunny seems to have a lot of influence on him, and I don't think she will allow him to help.

"Hol, trust me."

Trust him? He has some nerve even suggesting that. "I've trusted you before, Owen, and look how that turned out."

"How can you say something like that?" he asks, looking hurt. I stay quiet. "Listen, I know I made mistakes."

I burn with anger at his words. I don't want to hear them. "Mistakes? You repeatedly promised you'd stop gambling, and you broke it every time. I don't need your promises. Do you know how long it's taken me to rebuild my life? I'm still working on it."

His face sours, and he turns around, leaving without another word.

A tangle of junk spills out of my purse and skitters across the kitchen table. "Holly, what is the matter with you? What did that table ever do to you?" My mom picks up my purse and hangs it on a hook in the breezeway. "You're awfully testy today."

I pull out a chair and sink into it. "It was a long day, but that's not what upset me right now."

"I can tell. That bump against the table was like an explosion. I figured something had to have set you off."

"Do you want to talk about it?"

I think about opening up to her, but immediately shut down that thought. "That's okay. I'm just feeling frustrated right now."

She puts her hand on mine and leans toward me. Her perfume smells like gardenias. "If you ever want to talk about it," she says in a soothing voice, "I'm here."

The warmth of her hand brings a sense of peace, if only for a moment. If she even had a clue who I was frustrated with, she'd have my head. "Anything new here?"

My mom's eyes light up like Christmas morning. "Actually," she says and takes a seat across from me. "Do you remember Carol Kent?"

I wrack my brain, trying to picture her. I can only think of Clark Kent, and I know she is not talking about Superman. I shake my head. "Doesn't ring a bell."

"That's fine." She waves her hand at me. "I used to work with Carol. She's around fifteen years younger than me and started her own marketing firm."

"Good for her," I say, more because my mother is looking at me like I should say something than because I have anything particular to add. Why would I care what Carol Kent has been doing?

"Stop it, Holly. I'm going somewhere with this."

"Sorry." I stop fidgeting with my hands and rest them on my lap. "I didn't know."

"Well, now you do. Anyway, she started this firm about three years ago and recently moved into a building on Penrose Street."

My heartbeat quickens. Penrose Street? That was the premier spot in Helmlock for businesses. Well, as premier as any place in Helmlock could be. Big office buildings lined the streets, from law firms to marketing to interior design. Helmlock may be a small town, but that is a booming place to be if you aren't going to be in the heart of Milwaukee.

"Wow, that's pretty cool."

"Right? She sent me pictures of the inside, and it's so amazing."

I'm waiting for this story's point because there must be one. I mean, that's great for Carol Kent and all, but how does this relate to me?

"When she emailed me the pictures, she asked about you."

"She did?"

"Yes! When we worked together, I told her about you and

Vivienne. She remembered that you have a degree in graphic design. She wants to add a designer to her team!" My mom beams with excitement, a radiant smile brightening her face and eyes.

"Oh, that's... interesting." I can feel my face twist into one of my usual "What does this have to with me" half-smiles. My mom loves opportunities, especially those she can shove in my direction. Her eyes soften like she can read my mind and knows exactly how annoyed I am.

"Holly, you don't want to live with your mom and dad forever. This is the perfect opportunity for you to move on and do something else, something with your degree. What if this is your big break calling your name right now?" Her words rush out until she finally stops to take a breath, and the coffee maker percolating fills the silence.

"Wait. You want me to call her about a job?"

My mom shakes her head. "No. You don't have to. She wants you to come in on Monday for an interview! I've already set it up!"

She's beaming with pride as though she's put an end to war in the world. "You what?"

"I set it up! I told her you'd be so excited. I wrote down all the information and put it on your desk in your room. She just needs you to email her to confirm. What do you think?"

"What do I think?" What do I *think*? On the one hand, I can't believe my mom went ahead and set all this up for me without asking what I wanted. On the other hand, the simple thought of doing something I love and getting out of that grocery store makes me giddy.

"Well?"

"I'm thinking."

"What is there to think about?" My mom asks. "This is it, Holly. So much good can come from this. I want you to be happy." She smiles at me as she brushes her long, graying hair behind her ears, revealing a soft face worn by time and stress beyond its years.

"I *am* happy." The words come out, but I am not sure I mean them. Am I content? Sure. Life is what it is right now. I have a roof over my head and a job. Am I really happy, though? I don't know.

My mom's eyes narrow. "Holly, come on," she says. "I don't doubt how great you are at your job. You are a great manager. I know it, and you know it. I can see it on your face when you talk about your job. This isn't what you want to be doing. You're stuck."

I can't tell if that was a backhanded comment, or a poorly phrased observation. "I'm making money, though, and that's what's important."

"It's not all about money. Yes, if you took a job with Carol, you would make more than at the grocery store. But it's so much more than that. You're talented and don't have any opportunities to use that talent in your current job. You're the store manager now. There isn't anywhere to go from there."

Her words sting, but she's making a valid point. I had reached the highest level possible at the store and I wasn't sure how I could go further. If I wanted to, I could work for the corporate office, which would mean moving to the city. And it wasn't like I was going to become a Super Manager or something like that. That job didn't exist.

"Are you worried about succeeding like your sister was with her store? Does doing well scare you?"

"No, nothing like that." When Vivienne opened her store, Exquisite by Viv, success scared her. And her boyfriend, Cal, put up some of the money. She didn't know what it would do to their relationship. It's been great, though, and she's running a fabulous business with multiple employees now. I wanted to work for her, but as much as we love each other, we didn't think mixing family into the business would be a good idea.

"What, then?"

"You don't understand, Mom. So much has changed with graphic design since I graduated. I can't possibly compete with those coming right out of college. I'll be a fish out of water. There's no sense in getting my hopes up if I'm not even sure I will get past a first interview."

My mom rubs her hand on the table in a circular motion. "Oh honey, I understand if you're happy where you are. But I also know you can do so much better."

She stands up, pushes her chair in, and crosses her arms. "This is your decision." She pauses to take a breath. "I can't make it for you. But please think it through before you email Carol to cancel. I really believe that this is worth it. You know that I support you."

Mom kisses my forehead and wishes me good luck, leaving me to make a complicated decision I'm not sure I can.

❄   2 4   ❄

I arrive early to work on Saturday, and it's already snowing when I get out of my car. Big, soft flakes float down, blanketing the parking lot in a thick layer of powder. At first, the lot is pristine. But as I leave the store at the end of my shift, that's not the case. The entrance and exit ways are clear, but every car parked along the side of the building has a drift in front, nearly up to their windows.

I brush away the snow on the windshield of my car. I have to scrape the ice off. When finished, my door handle is frozen shut, and I have to dig my glove into the metal to free it. Snow crystals find their way to my seat when I open the door. I sit down, my butt quickly wet from the snow.

After I press the button, the engine hums, and a few moments later, the seat warmer turns on. Holiday songs start blasting through the speakers. I close my eyes for a moment as the hot air from the vent blasts into my face. "Jingle Bells" is playing, and I'm immediately transported to my grade school holiday concerts.

The snow starts picking up again. I glance out my window

and see a woman walking toward me from a white Cadillac Escalade. It's Crystal Silver, my boss, and she's motioning for me to roll down the window. I flick the switch with my finger, and the window slides down.

"Hello, Ms. Silver. What are you doing out in this storm?"

"Business as usual," she says. "Can you please meet me in the office?"

"I have to get going." I glance at the clock on my dash. It's after five. I want to get home, change, and see Levi. He's picking me up for dinner, so I don't have to drive in this storm. It will be good to see him after a hard day of work; frankly, that's all that got me through today.

Her lips are drawn tight, and her face is pinched and hard. "This is rather important, she says."

I hesitate. I can't say no, though, and she knows that. "Fine. I'll be right in. Just give me a minute."

I break into a sweat, and my heart races as I watch Crystal hurry into the store. What is this about now? Is she promoting Scottie to the manager now? Does she want me to create a shrine dedicated to her son? Both annoyed and scared, I text Levi, telling him I'm running late and will text again when I get home.

Once back inside the store, I make a beeline for the office. I want to get whatever this is over with and head back home. I have the next three days off and am anxious to start this mini-vacation.

Crystal is seated at the desk when I arrive, staring at me intently. Her hair is tied back, lips pursed in a tight frown, watching me with a sharp gaze. Her voice floats across the room. "Shut the door, Holly."

I shut the door, and the walls start closing in on me. My mind shuffles through a thousand different scenarios that made her request my presence after I've clocked out.

"Is everything okay?" I take my time sitting in the chair across from her.

She pushes her sleeves up and clasps her hands together. Her eyes are steady, boring into me. "If everything was okay, Holly, would I have called you in here?"

My cheeks burn with embarrassment. "I guess not."

Crystal rolls her chair back, retrieves a plastic bag from the bottom drawer, and then tosses it onto the desk.

"What am I looking at?" I ask.

"These are marijuana cigarettes."

"Marijuana cigarettes? You mean joints?"

"You'd know the terminology, wouldn't you?"

"Wait, you think this is mine?" I would *never* smoke weed at work. The few times I've gotten high, I took gummies. Joints aren't my style.

"I found them in *your* drawer. While some think marijuana should be allowed, it's still illegal in Wisconsin and not welcome in my store."

"It's not mine. I've never seen it before in my life."

"A likely story."

"Ms. Silver, I'm telling you the truth." I'm pleading with her to believe me.

"I'm sorry, Holly, but the evidence is there. I can't have you bringing this into the workplace. You're fired."

The words linger in the air like the sickly sweet order of overripe fruit. My lungs fill with a sense of dread. "I'm what?"

"Fired. Effective immediately. I'm glad Scottie brought this to my attention."

"Scottie?" I spat. "He told you about this?" My hands clench into fists, and I feel like my fingers might break if I squeeze harder. We share the desk, and Crystal knows that. It's either Scottie's, or he planted it there—or both.

"Ms. Silver, please," I hold my hands up in a prayer position. "It isn't mine, I swear. I need this job. The other day Scottie was in here—"

"Scottie? Are you suggesting my son had something to do with this?" A glimmer of rage flashes in her eyes.

That's exactly what I'm suggesting, and she knows it. "Yes."

"You don't have the right to accuse my son of such a thing."

I jump up and cross my arms over my chest. "What gives you the right to accuse *me*? If you don't recall, Scottie is now an assistant manager and shares that desk with me."

"Scottie wouldn't do this." She's shaking her head, and I think she truly believes what she's saying.

"I've done a great job managing this store. I help out when I'm not even asked, work overtime, and never complain. This place would fall apart without me!"

Crystal stands up now. "I built this business." She pushes her finger into her chest. "We were doing fine before you came along, and we'll do fine after. Get the hell out of my store before I call the police." She's pointing at the door, her face red with anger.

I'm tempted to tell her Scottie stole from the store—*her* store. I can pull examples of his deception and corrupt ways from every angle in this room. But I won't. Instead, I take my key card and store keys out of my pocket and slam them on the desk. I open the door with an aggressive pull and pump my arms as I shuffle through the store.

Nora tries to stop me, but I'm not halting for anyone. The sliding doors open for me, and I step through them as an unemployed female with more debt than she can handle. My shoulders have never felt so heavy.

The wind hits my face, and it feels like it's scraping it raw. I try to take shelter in my jacket, but that doesn't work. The air is freezing, cutting and clawing at my skin. My eyes start watering, but it's not from the frigid air. I don't see my car, and then I realize I *do* see it. It's buried under a pile of snow the plow had pushed there.

A shitty end to a shitty day.

❧ 2 5 ❧

I can't believe I'm standing on Penrose Street. The street is lined with lamps decorated with bright ribbons, lights, and bows. The smell of pine needles and balsam fills the air as the neighborhood is covered in Christmas cheer.

The grocery store was the only job I've ever held, and now that I've been let go, I find myself mustering up the courage to interview with my mom's friend, Carol. Working full-time right after college outside of my chosen field didn't give me any skills with which to expand my resume. I don't know what I'm doing here.

Surviving. That's what I'm doing. If I have to bullshit my entire way through this interview, that's what I must do.

I crank my neck to put the entire building in view, the number 46 in the center of the revolving door giving way to its address—46 Penrose Street. The snow crunches beneath my feet as I cross the street. I go through the revolving doors, almost revolving myself all the way back outside, but I find my strength and continue to the lobby.

The first thing my eyes are drawn to when I enter are the

walls. They gleam like polished granite with silvery veins and are etched with an impressionist depiction of Lake Michigan at sunset. The floors are a mirror-finished tile, the spaces between them filled with crushed aluminum flakes. The black plaque on the wall lists the firm names and their offices in gold lettering.

Carol's firm is listed high on the chart, so I have to pull my head back to see the floor. I find it and push the button to the elevator. When the doors open, I can't believe how fancy the inside is. It matches the ambiance of the rest of the building perfectly. I hope I'm not underdressed in my pencil skirt and cornflower blouse. Viv assured me this was the outfit to impress, but now I wonder if a pantsuit would have been a better option.

Too late now.

I grip the handle of the briefcase my father lent me. The black leather is worn and cracked, fraying at the edges where I grasp it. I needed something to appear more professional. Perhaps a worn-out briefcase wasn't the best idea.

The elevator doors open into a large area with marble floors like the main level, chandeliers, and tall windows along one wall that look out onto the cityscape. I head to the front desk, where a woman with dark curls and cherry-red lipstick sits behind a computer.

"Good morning. My name is Holly James. I have an appointment with Carol Kent."

The woman stands, and I shake her hand. "I'm Allison Blake. I'll let Carol know you're here."

"Thank you." I sit in an oversized charm with colorful geometric shapes and smooth fabric. The view out the window is full of dark clouds, suggesting another possible round of snow.

The wall to my left is full of different paintings. I don't have any time to absorb them because Allison calls me to

Carol's office. I smooth down my skirt and pick up my briefcase.

I walk through the doorway and immediately feel at ease. Carol stands from her desk and smiles at me. Her bright green dress shines against her chestnut skin.

"Welcome, Holly. Please have a seat." She points to a chair by the window. I'm in awe as I sit, the area below a winter wonderland. I spot a few walking trails transformed with decorated trees.

"Beautiful, isn't it?"

Her voice pulls me out of my trance. I could get used to this every day. "Yes, it is. How do you get anything done?"

"I manage." She sits and folds her hands in front of her. "Now, the reason you're here. You're interested in working at Kent Illuminations."

I try to find the right words. My mouth feels dry, but I lick my lips and mentally prepare. I try to look confident. "Well, my mom said you had an opening and thought I would be a good fit." My voice catches in my throat; it sounds terrible.

"Yes, she had wonderful things to say about you. Why do *you* think you'd be a good fit here?"

I start to answer her when I realize I have given it very little thought. The first rule of a job interview is preparation, and I've failed. I'll never get this job. The anticipation of a steady income is all I saw.

"I have a bachelor's degree in graphic design from UW-Madison, which I earned roughly sixteen years ago. I know design has changed tremendously over the years, and people can make truly stunning campaigns these days."

"Have you done any design work lately?"

"I haven't. I draw in my notebook and play a little on the computer. Honestly, though, I'm behind in the times when it comes to the newest software." If I haven't blown it already, this will surely seal my fate.

Carol throws her head back in laughter. Her eyes crinkle and sparkle when she laughs. "Holly, these days, the minute a program is released, it's practically obsolete. It all moves so quickly." She clasps together as she speaks. "Let me tell you about what I'm doing at Kent Illuminations. I'm building a team of strong, successful women to take the world of graphic design and marketing to an entirely different level. I believe in your mom's intuition, and I believe in my own. I think you'll fit in here."

She hasn't even seen a portfolio. How can she know that? "Ms. Kent—"

"Please call me Carol."

"Okay, Carol. I don't think I have the expertise a company of your caliber needs."

"I appreciate you saying so. You may not have it now, but you can obtain it. You can learn on the job, but if you're interested, I can send you to a couple of classes that will help."

As I listen, a sense of panic fills my chest. Is she offering me a job *plus* the opportunity to go to school? I can't ask her to do that.

"Thank you, but I can't."

"Why not? Give me one good reason."

I'm void of an answer and in disbelief at the offer. Why is she extending this opportunity to me? Do I deserve this?

"Holly, don't overthink it. If you want the job, it's yours. Just say yes."

I sit there considering everything she's said and offered to me. If I don't take this chance, I'm a fool.

I nod.

❧ 26 ❧

I can't believe I'm at the bar on a Monday night. I went from fired to hired in a matter of days, and I'm celebrating! We're at The Copper Fig, the perfect place for a celebration: dim lights, soft music, and many smiling faces. I sip on my margarita with my arm looped around Levi's. My friends are finally meeting him.

"Finally! We meet the man himself!" Dani's enthusiasm, though not surprising, is something I should have warned Levi about. "We've never met anyone from Holly's childhood. Well, except for Viv, but that's because they are sisters. What was she like when she was little? Was she as annoying then as she is now?" Dani flings her arm around me, and I shrug her off and tighten closer to Levi.

"No, she's not." Levi kisses my cheek. "She's sweet."

I hope that no one can see me blushing. "I only annoy Viv because that's my job as her younger sister."

"That's right! Let me assure you that she exceeds expectations, too. I wouldn't have it any other way, though."

With a slow deep breath, Levi flexes his arm. I'm sure the mention of sibling rivalry hits his heart in the most painful way imaginable, as if a small army of javelins pierces through his heart.

"So Viv," Levi says as he loosens up. "Holly mentioned that you own your own business."

Viv beams brightly. "I do," she says, nodding. "It's called Exquisite by Viv, a personal shopping venture. It was a big gamble—" Viv pauses and looks at me, knowing the word gamble is a bit of a trigger word for me. "—This is my calling, though," she continues. "I've never been happier."

"That suits you. I remember in middle school, you had quite the style."

Viv laughs. "Back then, maybe you thought so, but think back to the stuff we used to wear. It was hideous!"

"Oh, I recall. I specifically remember a pair of bright pink jelly shoes Holly used to wear. She rolled her jeans and teased her bangs. I even remember this pair of earrings she had that were daisies."

"I loved neon colors and huge hoop earrings!" Sadie jumps in.

"For me," Viv says, "I loved belts. I had this one from Delia's that was bright sunflowers. I wore my stone-washed jeans with it and paired them with a black crop top. Oh my gosh, I must have looked like such a nerd." She covers her face with her hand.

"I bet it was cute." Her boyfriend, Cal, comes up behind her and kisses her neck.

"Honey! What are you doing here? I thought you had to work late tonight."

"I managed to finish early, and I thought I'd surprise you." Cal shoots a hand out toward Levi. "I'm Cal. Nice to meet you."

"Levi." They shake hands, and Viv gives me a look that says she's excited the men in our lives have met. I'm sure she's many double dates in our future.

"Does Joe have Rose tonight?" Cal asks Sadie.

"Yep. Mama needs a break. Besides, he left me for almost a week to go deer hunting at the beginning of November. He can handle a few hours," Sadie jokes. Joe is an amazing dad and would do anything for Rose. Any of us here would.

"Levi, tell us about yourself." Sadie jumps in again, bringing her teacher out of her. Next, she'll have him write a three-page essay about his favorite animal.

"Like what?"

"Likes, dislikes, how much you adore Holly."

"Sarcasm, mean people, and more than she can ever know," Levi answers in order.

My heart quickens at his response. I don't know if anyone has ever said they've *adored* me.

"How about your favorite Christmas movie? Don't say *Die Hard*." Dani jokes. She argues with Joe about this all the time. He loves *Die Hard,* and Dani hates it. Sadie doesn't dare get in the middle.

"My favorite Christmas movie." Levi scratches the top of his head. "It's a toss-up between *Home Alone* and *Gremlins*."

"*Gremlins*? How is *that* a holiday movie? I haven't seen it for years, but I can only remember the mogwai. I think his name was Gizmo."

"The movie's entire premise is the father giving his son a Christmas present. There's snow, carolers. It has it all!"

"Holly, your favorite is *The Nightmare Before Christmas*. I still don't know if that is a Halloween or Christmas movie," says Viv. She sips her mojito and smiles.

"The word *Christmas* is in the title! And Tim Burton is amazing. You're all obsessed with *Love, Actually*. No, thank you." I don't mind the movie. I really like it. But I don't want to fall into the same category as everyone else. I like to be a bit different.

Levi falls into place with my friends as though he's been a

part of our group the entire time. Sure, it helps that he's known Viv and me for such a long time, even if most of that time we've been separated. Besides the mention of sibling rivalry before, Levi seems to be in a better place, and his mood isn't altered because of Amy. I think he's having fun.

We move the party over by the dartboard, and it's not long before Viv is kicking my butt. She's always been the more sporty of us, even with something like this. We're playing a game of 301. She only needs an eight to win, and I'm still hovering around ninety-nine.

"This is *not* a close game."

The dart flies out of my hand when I hear Owen's voice behind me. It embeds in the wall, and a piece of drywall flutters to the ground. I spin around.

"Owen. What are you doing here?"

"I stopped by your parent's house, and your dad said you weren't home. I figured you'd be here. He's not too happy with me, is he?"

I'm sure my father wasn't too pleased to see him. Owen made it to The Copper Fig in one piece, so he must have been somewhat civil toward him. "What do you want?" I don't know what to think after our last conversation.

"Yeah, Owen, what do you want?" Dani pushes her sleeves to her elbows like she's ready to take him down. He better be careful because Dani *does* have karate training.

Owen stands there, not even looking up at Dani as she comes close. He tilts his head to the side and opens his mouth wide. "Settle down." He holds his hands up as if to show he's not carrying any weapons, not realizing words can be weapons, too.

"Is this the new boyfriend?" He points to Levi, unimpressed. "Hey, guy, I'm Owen, Holly's ex-husband."

Levi doesn't respond, but his jaw is clenched so tight I'm afraid he may break his teeth.

"Wow. Tough crowd here today."

"We don't want you here." Sadie shocks me with her bluntness. She's not huge on confrontation, but since she had Rose, her confidence has skyrocketed. Plus, all of us protect each other. "I think you should leave."

"I'm hurt." He touches his hands to his heart. "I didn't think you hated me that much. Besides, Holly's the one who broke into my apartment, not the other way around."

"Dude, just say what you came to say so the ladies can continue their game." Levi stands in front of me, blocking Owen from my view.

"Okay, okay. No need to go all Rocky on me." He steps around Levi. "Holly, I might have an idea where that charm is."

"Are you being serious?" I can't deal with him playing jokes on me. "Don't mess with me."

"Yes, I'm serious."

"Where is it?" I ask impatiently. "You said you knew where it was."

"I *think* I know where it is," Owen says. "I want you to help me find it."

There is pleading in his eyes, and he stares at me while all I hear is Olivia Rodrigo's "*Good 4 U*" playing in the background. I feel everyone watching us, waiting for me to say something. I don't know how to respond, though. I want this charm, but I don't have much of a desire to spend time with Owen.

"Let's go talk outside." I push past Levi and my friend and beat Owen outside. I'm freezing without my jacket.

"Your friends hate me, don't they?"

"You're not their favorite person." Nor mine, but I don't say that.

"Can't they move on?"

"No!" A couple passing by glances when I yell and move

closer to the sidewalk's edge. "No," I say, quieter. "You left me in so much debt, Owen. My life has veered off track because of you. If it weren't for my parents, I wouldn't even have my head above water."

He wants to say something. Maybe apologize. Or blame me for everything that happened. He opens his mouth to say something, but closes it and starts again. "About the charm. I don't know what I am looking for. I need your help if I'm going to find it."

Owen is the only chance I have of finding the charm. Once I find it, I never have to see him again.

"Fine. I can come tomorrow night at six."

"Sunny will be home."

"I don't care. She can either help or stay the hell out of my way. Got it?" I'm calling the shots this time. It may be risky, but from the strain in his eyes, I can tell he knows I mean business.

He swallows hard as the wind howls. "Got it," he says.

27

Levi insists on coming with me to Owen's. That's fine because I'm not entirely comfortable going by myself. Besides, if Sunny will be there, then maybe having Levi with me will help bridge the gap with that awkwardness.

Levi made spaghetti for us as an early dinner. I want to have a full stomach so I can concentrate. Hunger will only make me irritable, and I don't think it's wise to increase my level of that right now.

"If you don't mind me asking, and if I'm out of line, say so, but what exactly happened with Owen? I know he had a gambling addiction, and that caused your relationship to end."

I twirl a few noodles onto my fork. "He promised to stop dozens of times. Finally, I had enough and filed for divorce. We had joint accounts; he even opened things in my name without my knowledge to draw money against. As a result, I incurred a lot of his debt. That forced me to move in with my parents to pay it off. Eventually, I will, but I don't see that happening soon."

"I'm sorry. That's terrible. Were you married long?"

"No. It was only a few years since we met, married, and divorced. Had I taken the time to get to know him better, maybe I wouldn't be in this position."

"You can't blame yourself," Levi says, reaching across the table for the little bowl of grated parmesan cheese.

I shake my head. "I did for a while. I don't anymore. When I realized how bad the problem had gotten, I suggested he attend a gambling addiction group. He didn't go. I refused to live in debt, so I left. Little did I know the debt followed me."

"Hopefully, with this new job, you can climb out of debt sooner than expected."

"I hope so. I'm so grateful for my parents allowing me to live with them rent-free. One day I'll repay them. But being almost forty and living with my parents isn't the dream I imagined for myself."

He takes a sip of his wine. "I don't think most of us live the lives we imagined for ourselves."

He's probably right. When I was younger, I wanted to marry Johnny Depp and live in a villa in France. Part of me probably thought that was attainable when I was young. "No? What did you imagine?"

His eyes glisten, and dimples appear as he chuckles. "I thought I'd be living near the beach playing professional baseball."

I visualize him in a baseball uniform, stepping up to home plate. His uniform clings to his body in a sheen of sweat, his muscles bulging in his arms.

"Life had other plans, though," he says, interrupting my fantasy. "That's okay. I'm happy with where I am."

A handsome man has made me dinner. I start a new job on Monday, and digging myself out of debt may be sooner than I think. "Me, too," I say.

Levi reaches across the table and puts his hand on top of mine. For a moment, the world falls away. We're the only ones left in the universe.

"We should go," he says as he pulls his hand back. "You told Owen you'd be there at six, and it's a quarter to."

I wish we didn't have to go. I want to stay here. But I want to find the charm so I can put closure on my past.

Twenty minutes later, we're standing outside Owen's apartment. He opens the door and looks like a complete mess. His hair is matted to his head, the strands frayed and wispy. His eyes are bloodshot, and his shirt is partially buttoned and wrinkled in places.

"Holly, what are you doing here? And what's this guy here with you for?" He points to Levi.

"You're kidding, right?"

"Um, no." He scratches his head. "Did you forget something the night you broke into my place?"

"Did you forget I'm here to help you look for the charm? You said you need my help to find it."

He laughs. "Oh, yeah. I was a little drunk last night. And this morning. I completely forgot."

"Drunk?"

He leans into me. "Hammered."

His breath reeks of a night of drinking whiskey and smoking cigarettes. When did he take up smoking?

"Sunny quit the computer shop and then moved her stuff out. I had a drink. Then another and another. I tore apart the apartment because I was so pissed. That's when I found the charm."

"Wait." I take hold of Levi's hand and squeeze. "You found it?"

"A plastic, yellow boombox thing, right? Real cheesy. I found it and put it in my pocket. Then I came to your house, and you were at The Copper Fig."

"Owen, did you have it when you saw me last night?"

He belches loudly. "Yep." A hiccup follows. "Then I saw you with this loser," he thumbs over to Levi, "and decided maybe I don't want you to have this charm."

My heart is pounding so hard against my chest it hurts. "It means nothing to you," I say, my throat closing.

"Right. It doesn't. But it *does* mean something to you."

I don't care for his smarmy, condescending tone. I want to smack him across the face.

"Where is it?" Levi asks with a scowl.

"Levi, that's your name, right? You're named after a brand of blue jeans." He chuckles and sings the jingle. He reaches into the pocket and pulls out the charm. I try to snatch it when he dangles it, but he pushes my hand away. "Not so fast."

"Come on, Owen." There's no reasoning with him. Not when he's this drunk. Maybe we'd be better off if we let him sleep it off and come back. "Don't be like this."

"Like what?" Owen asks, leaning against the door frame, more to keep himself up than to try to look like he's in control.

"A dick," Levi hisses, sharp and cutting.

"You better watch it, dude. I'll knock you out flat with one punch." He takes one step, stumbles, and his arms flail backward. He manages to catch himself against the door frame.

Levi doesn't even budge. "Is that right? You don't appear to be in any position to throw anything, much less a punch."

I stare at Levi's fist, and he's tightened it. I speak softly, but my voice is still firm. "Don't do this, guys. Owen, please give me the charm."

"So, what are you offering me?"

"Excuse me?"

"This charm." He takes it out, twirls it around for me to

see, and then shoves it back into his pocket. "What's it worth to you?"

"You wouldn't." I saw through gritted teeth.

"I'm a bit low on cash. Maybe three hundred dollars?"

"Three hundred dollars? Are you kidding me?" I yell. The cold air is bitter and hurts my lungs. "Thanks to you, I don't have extra money to spare." And even if I did, I don't think I'd give him any of it. He'll gamble it away.

"Okay, there has to be some other way to do this," Levi jumps in. His tone has changed. "Can't you find it in your heart to give the charm back to Holly? It's not yours. It never was."

"But it *is* on my property. I need money, and this is a way I can get it. I'm all about seizing opportunities."

"Not gonna happen," Levi says. He arches like a giant sequoia and crosses his arms in defiance. "Hand it over, and you'd better do it fast before I get angry."

"The only way that's happening is if you forcibly take it from me."

"Try me."

"Levi, don't, please." I implore him. He turns to me, his eyes running over my face, searching.

Owen grows impatient. "Do you want to do this over some stupid plastic piece of crap? What's so important about this, anyway?"

I can't help but feel my heart clench when Owen calls the charm stupid. The memory of all the times we traded the necklace, excited to see which charm was next to claim its place on the chain, comes rushing back, filling my heart with sadness.

I can't stand here and listen to him berate the charm.

"You wouldn't understand, and I'm not explaining it to you." Chances are Owen won't remember most of this conversation tomorrow, anyway. "Let's go, Levi. I'll figure this out some other way."

Levi's eyes dart back and forth, looking into mine, searching for a response. "Are you sure? I'll stand here all night until we get what we came for, if that's what you want."

I glance between my past and my future. What Owen holds in his pocket is important to me, but I can't give him that kind of money. Not right now. And if I do, well, that's only enabling his addictions. I don't want to be that person.

Amy will always be with me, even if I never retrieve the charm. I may not have the charm, but I have the letter, and now Levi. Maybe that's all I need.

I swallow hard as I make the decision. "I'm sure."

"Fine." He turns back to Owen. "You're lucky. Tonight. Don't think this is over."

As we start walking away, Owen slurs, "She brought this on herself, you know. If she hadn't acted like such a little bi—"

There's no time for me to stop him. Levi is a freight train barreling toward Owen. Levi slams his fist into Owen, and Owen hits the ground hard.

"Levi! What are you doing?" I'm pulling Levi back from the apartment as Owen struggles to stand. People start coming out of their apartments. I notice someone on the phone, probably calling the police.

"I'm sorry, Holly. I'm not going to stand for him calling you something like that."

"It's a name, Levi." He's probably called me worse than that before. "It doesn't hurt me."

Police sirens blare in the distance. I wonder if they're coming to the apartment building or if it's a coincidence. Levi appears panicked.

"Serves you right," Owen says as he stands, his nose bleeding. "I think you might have broken my nose."

"Good." Levi backs up against the wall. "I'll just wait here for the police, then."

"I can't believe you did that," I say to Levi, ignoring Owen and his bloody nose. "Hitting someone is never the way to respond, as much as you'd like to sometimes. You can wait here. I'll be in the car and give the police my statement when they get here."

I stomp away and don't bother looking back.

❧ 28 ❧

"Thanks for doing this," Dani says as she puts the hat on my head. "I want to make sure this is perfect." I cross my arms as she fiddles with the hat, her long, thin fingers plucking and tugging at it.

"Yeah, no problem," I say as I stand in front of the full-length mirror. The thick wool of the hat itches my head. I try to scratch at it, but Dani stops me.

"The hat is perfect. Deal with it. This will take all of five minutes."

I sigh. I did promise I'd do this, so I have to do it her way. The local mall hired her to do Santa photos. Even though a winter wonderland will be set up, she's created her own in her home to practice. She wants to practice the angles and make sure everything is perfect.

I'm not in a festive mood, but I don't break my promises.

"Here." Dani holds something out to me. It's white, long, and curly.

"What the hell is that?"

"A fake beard because you look nothing like Santa Claus without it."

146

"I am *not* putting on a beard." I shake my head in disbe-lief. I don't see how the beard is necessary for this. It won't make or break the pictures.

"You have to."

"No, I don't," I say as I look back at myself in the mirror. "But I will." I snatch the beard out of her hand and put it on, immediately drawing a laugh from her.

"Do you want me to take it off?" I threaten, tugging at the coarse white hair.

"No! I'm sorry. I appreciate the help."

I'm not being fair to Dani. She's trying to do her job, and I'm making it hard on her. "I'm out of it, that's all."

Dani takes me by the arm and props me next to the over-sized chair in her studio. The backdrop is a white wall with a tree in the corner decorated with small ornaments. The room smells of pine and a hint of peppermint, which is soothing.

"What's going on with you?" She asks as she takes some shots with her camera and then adjusts the lighting. I only take photos with my phone, so I admire her work. She's very talented.

"Oh, nothing," I answer, as though it is no big deal. "Levi went with me to Owen's to search for the charm and ended up punching him out."

"Excuse me, what?" Dani clutches the camera to her chest. "Levi did *what*?"

"You heard me. He punched out Owen, who had drunk his weight in booze." I've seen Owen drunk before, but never like he was that night.

"Good for him. Owen probably deserved it."

There had been plenty of times Dani probably wanted to deck Owen herself. I'm not shocked she is happy someone finally did it.

"Maybe, but that doesn't make it a good decision." I can't stop thinking about the spectacle. Sure, I felt a tingling sense of justice, but no matter how much debt Owen put me in, he didn't deserve that. He could barely stand. "Levi is lucky that Owen didn't press charges. When all was said and done, I told Levi to call himself an Uber, and I went home."

"You left him there?"

"He's a big boy. I couldn't deal with it."

Dani adjusts my shoulders so I face the front of the room. "Did you at least find the charm?"

"No. Actually, Owen *has* it. He had it when he came to The Copper Fig the other night. He wants money for it."

Dani's cheeks are turning red. "That asshole," she says, her voice rising. "He can't charge for that when it's not even his!"

"Well, he's trying and says it's the only way I'll get it back." I think back to him struggling to hold himself up before Levi punched him. "He's in a bad place, Dani."

She backs up and snaps a few pictures. "Not your problem."

I yank the beard down, grateful to have the itchy material off my face. "What if it is, though? Did I give up on him too easily?"

Dani takes a knee next to me. "No. Don't talk like that. You gave that man everything, and he refused when you tried to help him. That's on *him*, not on you. Got it?"

I did try. You have to put the work into marriage, and I did that. But when we said our vows, we promised in sickness and in health, for richer or poorer. Did *I* break my vows by leaving after he refused to help himself?

I try to speak, but my voice cracks. I blink furiously, trying to stem the tears. Santa isn't supposed to cry. "If I'd stayed, maybe he would've gotten help, and we could've paid off our debts together."

"Sure." Dani stands and adjusts her camera strap. "And you'd be miserable. You weren't happy, Holly. We all could see that. You made the right choice. You're not responsible for Owen and the choices he makes. He's a grown man." She taps her foot against mine. "Well, kind of," she laughs.

"You're right. I just hate that he's turned into this despicable human being."

"Don't put him in the same category as the Minions, please. Besides, you're a people pleaser. I'm not at all surprised you're feeling this way. Holly, he's holding that charm hostage."

I didn't think of it like that. I'm not willing to give Owen any money, but at the same time, I don't want to make the situation worse. It's important to me that everyone wins in this situation. Why, though? Owen is keeping something important to me. He's refusing to allow me to have it. Why should I be so nice about it while he's being a jerk?

"What do I do, Dani? Maybe it's silly how badly I want the charm."

"If it means having a piece of Amy back, then it's not silly at all." She smiles tenderly. "You deserve to have it."

Her words mean everything to me now, providing an anchor when one is so badly needed. "How, though? How will I get it back?"

"I don't know, Holly. From what you told me happened the last time you saw him, I don't think he's willing to hand it over so easily."

That's the truth. Although if he's sober, he may be more likely to listen to reason.

Who am I kidding? I know Owen too well, and there is one way to get through to him. I don't like it, but it may be the only way.

"I think I know how I can get it back," I say. "Let's finish your pictures, and I'll fill you in."

❧ 29 ❧

The doorbell rings at the moment I'm falling into my father's recliner. I'm not much in the movie-watching mood, but I'm hoping a viewing of *The Nightmare Before Christmas* will put me in a better mood. Every time I think about Owen and the charm, or Levi and how he assaulted Owen, a headache blooms behind my eyes. I just want to relax for one night.

"I'll get it," my mom says, not bothering to pause the movie. She watches it with me so much I'm sure she knows the entire thing by heart.

A minute later, she returns to the room, beaming. "Holly, Levi is at the door. He has barely changed! I mean, he's taller and much more handsome, but I can still tell it's him!" She's beyond excited to see my childhood friend.

I didn't invite Levi over, so seeing him is a surprise. He texted me he wanted to talk, but I didn't reply. I assume this is why he popped over.

I set my bowl of popcorn on the table near my dad. Levi is waiting in the kitchen. "Levi, I wasn't expecting you."

He shrugs, his eyebrows arched. "Yeah, well... you're not responding to my texts."

I remain in the doorway across the kitchen with my arms crossed over my chest. My weight shifts to one leg, and I look at him with narrowed eyes. "That's because I didn't want to talk. Yet here you are."

"I'm sorry. I didn't mean to barge in."

"But you did."

"I thought you might miss me. I know I miss you." A smile curls across his face, and despite myself, I push my chin up a notch and return the smile. I'm still mad at him, but I can't resist those lips.

"Yes, I miss you. I just need some time." I uncross my arms and place them on my hips. "I can't believe you punched Owen."

"You knocked out Owen LaDolly?" My dad asks, striding into the room.

"Mr. James, hello." Levi holds out his hand, and my dad grabs it with a firm shake. He grasps Levi's arm in a two-handed pump up and down.

"It's nice to see you, son. It's been a long time." He pulls a chair out for Levi and motions for him to sit. "So what's this I hear about you hitting Owen?"

Levi clasps his hand together on the table. I notice his knuckles are slightly bruised. "It's not my proudest moment, Sir," he says.

My dad waves his hand at him. "He had it coming. Good for you."

"Dad! How can you say that?" I say in disbelief. "He could have been seriously hurt!"

I feel my blood boiling at my dad's callous words. How can he dismiss someone getting hit like that? It's not right.

My dad shrugs and chuckles. "Listen, Holly," he said. "Sometimes, you just have to stand up for yourself."

"You can't convince me that violence is the way to do that. I think it's childish."

"You're right." Levi scratches the back of his neck. "I'm sorry. Can you ever forgive me?"

My dad glances between Levi and me. "I'm going to get back to the movie. Good seeing you, Levi. Don't be a stranger."

Once my dad is out of the room, Levi stands and approaches me. The cologne he wears is fresh and inviting. I breathe him in, wanting to touch him, trace my fingers across his shoulders and down his arms. If I do, though, I may never let him go. I still don't forgive him.

"What do you say? Can you forgive me?"

His eyes sweep over me ask he asks for another chance. I know that who I saw at Owen's isn't Levi. They pushed each other's buttons until Levi had had enough. He should have walked away, but should've, would've, could've. What's done is done.

And I miss Levi terribly.

"If I forgive you"—his eyes light up like Christmas morning—"*if* I forgive you, that doesn't mean in any way I condone what you did to Owen. I think you made a terrible choice."

He shakes his head. "I know. I allowed Owen to get under my skin. Believe me when I say I have never hit anyone in my life. That charm belongs to you, but it's part of Amy, too. It kills me he's keeping it from you. It's like he's holding a piece of her hostage. Then when he called you that name, I lost it."

I feel my shoulders slump forward, and I look at the floor. "Damn, now *I* feel like a jerk," I say out loud. "I've been so caught up in getting the charm back that I never once considered how this affects you."

When he takes another step forward, I don't retreat. He places his hands on my shoulders and then runs them up my neck until he's cupping my face. "I don't think you're a jerk. Tell you what. If we're going to be jerks, let's be jerks together."

His hands, while they are cold, warm me inside. "You're cold."

"It's cold outside. I know what could warm me up." When his lips touch mine, I see stars dancing behind my eyes. His kiss tastes like cinnamon and honey, a sweet treat to savor on a cold night.

"Did that work?" I ask when our lips part.

"It sure did. Does this mean you forgive me?"

I smile, peace filling my body. "That depends. How do you feel about staying to watch The Nightmare Before Christmas with my parents and me?"

He unzips his thick black jacket, revealing a faded T-shirt printed with a picture of Jack Skellington. "What does this tell you?"

30

I kick off my heels as I unbutton my slacks. I pull them off and switch to my favorite pair of soft, faded jeans. The first week at Kent Illuminations has been a dream. Everyone is so friendly, and I love working with Carol. I can't believe I have my own office overlooking the city. Even though it's wintertime, the sun shines through the windows and warms me up. Such a welcome change from the tiny, cramped backroom at the grocery store.

"Are you sure you don't want me to go with you?" Levi is perched on the edge of my bed, a worry line creasing his forehead as I pull a sweater over my head.

"Absolutely. I don't think it's a good idea for you to go to that apartment."

"I understand, but I can't just stay away. I won't do anything to jeopardize the situation. I promise."

I quickly grab an elastic band and twist my hair into a tight ponytail. I toss my keys into my purse. "It's not happening," I say, my voice raising. "I'll text you every fifteen minutes. How does that sound?"

Levi's gaze roves the floor as he considers his options,

then meets mine with a resigned nod. "I guess I have no choice."

I wrap my hands around his neck and pull him close, pressing my lips against his. His breath hitches slightly, and I pull away with a smile. "I'll be back."

The entire drive over to Owen's, I keep questioning if I'm doing the right thing. I want the charm back, but am I playing into his weaknesses? Does it make me a bad person?

My hands grip the steering wheel as I pull into the parking lot. I glance in the rearview mirror, my heart pounding. Taking a few deep breaths, I step out of the car and stare at the apartment building. When I reach his unit, I knock lightly, my hand shaking.

The door creaks open. Owen stands there in silence, his face filled with apprehensiveness. I take a deep breath and say softly, "I'm sorry about what happened with Levi. It was out of line, and he knows it."

Owen studies me for a few moments before dropping his gaze. He takes a deep breath, then gives a slow nod. "It's okay," he mumbles. "I wasn't exactly innocent in that situation."

"I don't think it's fair that you're keeping that charm from me. I've come to take it back."

My heart races, expecting the door to be shut in my face. Instead, he widens the gap and gestures for me to enter. I step over the threshold and into his living room, my eyes shocked at what I'm seeing.

The apartment is *clean*. It looks nothing like what I saw the other day. The carpet is vacuumed, the kitchen counter is clear, and not a pizza box or dirty mug in sight. His clothes are neatly folded and placed in a laundry basket next to the spotless couch. He's even put up a Christmas tree. Not a fake one, either. The tree is a tad sparse but decorated nicely, and the pine smell permeates through the room.

"Impressed?" He asks, beaming with pride.

I shrug and say, "It's not like you deserve a medal." I am, of course, deeply impressed, but I don't want him to know that.

"Wow. I see you haven't lost your touch with sarcasm. And here I thought maybe I'd be nice and hand it over."

"That would be the easiest and kindest thing to do."

"It's for sale if you want it."

He glances away, nonchalantly adjusting the pillows on his couch.

I shrug one shoulder, pushing away a lock of hair that fell loose before taking a step forward. "May I take my jacket off?"

He seems surprised by the question, raising an eyebrow. "Oh, so you plan on staying awhile?"

I smile softly. "Not too long, but I'd like to be comfortable."

He gives a curt nod. "Then, by all means."

I take my jacket off and hang it on the hook next to the door. "I have a proposition for you."

"Oh?" Owen looks at me with hunger in his eyes, making my stomach do somersaults, bile rising in my throat.

"Ew. No."

"Ouch," he says. "Well, what is your proposition, then?"

I shift myself onto the couch. I tap my fingers against the armrest and meet Owen's gaze. "You want to play me for the charm?"

He crosses his arms and gives me a challenging look. "Holly James, are you asking me to gamble?"

My stomach drops, but I'm desperate. I don't know what else to do, so I nod my head slowly and say, "I guess I am."

"Alright then," he says. "If you win, then you get the charm. What do I get if *I* win?"

"You keep the charm. That's what we're playing for, after

all." This isn't a negotiation. I came in with the terms set. Simple as that.

"No, no. That's not how this works." He sits opposite me in the recliner, lengthening his seat to exert his power. "I already have the charm. You need to up the ante."

My lips are dry and chapped, so I lick them. I feel my pulse at my throat, my tongue as thick as the surrounding air.

Owen rubs his hands together. "You'll leave today with the charm, no matter what."

"I will?" Is it possible he's coming to his senses? Maybe I don't have to play for it.

"Well, that's up to you and how you want to play this. You can walk out that door with the plastic piece of crap if you win. If *I'm* victorious, I'll still give you the charm. But you have to give me five hundred dollars."

"Five hundred dollars!" I press my hands into the cushions so hard I'm sure they'll leave prints. The veins in my throat are throbbing. "I won it at the fair with a four-ticket play!"

"So it's worth a dollar, if even that. If it's that important to you, you'll do as I say." His eyes remain focused on me, and he clenches his jaw.

"Why are you doing this?" My voice wavers, but I stay strong.

He runs his fingers through his hair and shrugs. "Rent's due."

I'm frozen as I stare at this man before me, this man I once loved and once loved me. How had it come to this? How did he become someone willing to blackmail me? And how did I become an enabler again, using gambling to get what I want?

Do I have a choice, though?

"Fine. Deal." I reach my hand out, and we seal the deal with a handshake.

"Awesome. So, what's your game? Texas Hold 'Em? Black-jack? War?"

"Monopoly." If he flinches, I don't notice. Seven years ago, I competed in a state-wide Monopoly tournament. It's my game. I didn't win, but I made it to the top three.

"You want to hinge this on Monopoly?"

"Yes, I do. Are you afraid?" I lean closer, challenging him.

His face draws a smirk as he contemplates this. "Fine. Kitchen table. I'm the banker." He stands up and takes the game out of a closet near the kitchen.

I'm happy that we're playing a board game. It's been a while, and I really love them. When Owen and I were married, we played often when he was around, and we weren't arguing. Monopoly, Scrabble, Trivial Pursuit. We played them all.

I snatch the thimble, my standard piece. It had been retired for a while, but brought back after fans rallied for it. Owen is always the dog.

Huh. That seems appropriate now.

The game is slow to start. We take turns buying out all the properties and start building on them. We're a solid hour into the game when my phone buzzes. I ignore it, and it keeps buzzing every few minutes.

"Do you need to get that?"

"Nope." I silence my phone. I'm sure it's Levi. I never texted him like I said I would. I can't be distracted, though. When I play Monopoly, I need to be in the zone.

Forty-five minutes later, I'm slumped back in the chair, sighing heavily at the pile of colorful money and plastic houses strewn across the game board, most belonging to Owen. I'm left with Baltic Avenue and, even with a hotel on it, I can't possibly win this game.

"What happened?" I press my sweaty hand against my forehead. "You have never beat me."

Owen smiles. "Sunny liked playing. I got better. Don't be mad. *You* picked the game."

I let out an exasperated grunt, wishing I had chosen a game more suitable for my skills—like Tic-Tac-Toe.

"Don't be so sad, Holly. You can still take it home. Just fork over the money, and I'll hand it over."

My eyes burn as tears well up. The only sound is the heavy thud of my breaking heart. "I can't, Owen."

He pushes his chair back and stands. "What do you mean you can't?" he asks as if I haven't told him a thousand times.

"I mean, I can't. I don't *have* five hundred dollars to give you. Even if I did, I wouldn't. You need help, Owen. I thought you were in a better place, but you're not. The way you acted the other night and today. I'm ashamed of myself for even suggesting we gamble for the charm and even more so for actually doing it." I take my jacket from the hook and pull it on.

"Wait a minute," he says, his eyes narrowing. "Where are you going?"

I tighten my grip on the doorknob. "Home, Owen. I'm going home without the charm, and I won't bother you about it again."

He throws his hands in the air. "So, no money then?"

I laugh bitterly, my eyes still stinging. "No, Owen. No money. I wish I could give you something for it. All I want is this piece of me back. I have nothing to give you, though. Besides, giving you money is not a good idea, even if I had it."

Owen's brow furrows. "A piece of you? It's a little piece of plastic. Why is it such a big deal?"

My throat constricts as I explain the significance of the charm. "Because my best friend in grade school died, and that's one of the few pieces of her I have left."

His face softens, and his lips part, but nothing comes out.

He knows he made a mistake but doesn't know how to respond.

Empathy has never been one of his strong points.

I open the door and march away, my shoes tapping a broken rhythm against the pavement as I flee, not daring to look back even as he calls out my name.

The night air is cold, but nothing but hot anger courses through my veins.

31

By the time I arrive home from Owen's, I'm a complete mess. I try to wipe away the tears, but it's no use. My mascara has left dark smudges under my eyes, and strands of hair stick to my face. My parents look up from the kitchen table where Levi sits between them. I can't believe he's still here. I don't have the strength to explain what happened. I hurl past them, leaving a trail of salty tears in my wake.

"Holly." I hear Levi say my name as I slam my bedroom door so hard that a picture falls off the wall. I throw myself onto my bed. How is this happening?

I groan and bury my face in my pillow when I hear pounding on my door.

"Can I come in?"

"Go away, Levi," I call back. "I don't want to talk to anyone."

"Please. Tell me what happened."

Agitated, I shuffle to the door and pull it open. I glare at Levi with anger and tears in my eyes. "You happened, Levi," I hiss, gesturing wildly with my hands. "If you hadn't come back into my life, it wouldn't have drudged up all of these painful memories. I wouldn't be on a hunt for this charm. My life was perfectly fine without you in it."

The color in his face drains, and he frowns, but his eyes remain soft and full of love. "You don't mean that," he whispers with a hint of hope.

"I do, Levi," I say sadly, my voice cracking slightly. "Please, just leave."

He takes a deep breath as if he wants to say something.

"It's too hard, Levi. I tried so hard to move on after Amy died. She's all I've thought about since receiving your letter. Now I'm running around, breaking into my ex's apartment, and gambling with him for a plastic boombox I had all but forgotten about."

Levi looks into my eyes and speaks softly. "I understand it's hard for you. It's hard for me, too. But please, let's give this a chance. I won't give up on us."

I sigh heavily, my shoulders slumping. "I appreciate the sentiment, Levi," she says. "But this can't be fixed overnight. I can't make any promises." I look away, not wanting to meet his gaze.

Levi nods, understanding my reluctance. "I'll give you all the time you need. But please, let me prove that I'm worth a second chance. *We're* worth it." He takes a step back and turns away, leaving with a heavy heart.

My mom passes him in the hallway, and when she reaches my room, she reaches out to me. I don't want to be hugged, so she settles in on simply placing her hands on my arms. "What was that all about?" she asks, concern ringing in her voice.

I sink back into my bed, my body weighed down by exhaustion, sadness, and frustration. I can feel my mom's gaze fixed on me, even though I'm not facing her. She won't let this go until I explain what happened.

"Can't I just be alone?" I whisper, knowing she won't let that be the case.

"No. You need to explain why you stormed into the house and kicked Levi out. He cares about you, and it worried him when you didn't answer his texts."

She means well and only wants to help me. After all, my parents practically begged me to move back into their house so I can get out of debt. So, I swallow my pride and tell her everything.

My mom listens intently to my explanation and releases a deep sigh when I'm done. "Sweetheart." She rubs her hand in circles on my back like she used to when I was little. "You can't place all the blame on Levi."

I take a moment to process her words, feeling guilty for being so hard on Levi. The fact remains that a few weeks ago, I had been content with how life was. He has flipped it upside down. "If he hadn't contacted me, then none of this would have happened."

"That might be true," my mom says, her voice low, "but it doesn't change the fact that you still haven't come to terms with Amy's death."

The air in the room is still as we stare at each other. I swallow hard, pushing back the wave of emotion threatening to consume me. I can still picture the grief on my parent's faces when they told me Amy had lost her battle with cancer.

"What do you mean?" I ask, my voice small and fragile, as if it might crumple at the slightest touch.

"Your best friend died at thirteen years old. It's hard to make sense of death at any age, but it can be especially difficult as a teenager. You refused to leave your bedroom for days, sobbing until your voice was hoarse. And to my knowledge, you still haven't visited her gravesite. You're still carrying all this pain around with you.

"But if Levi hadn't—"

"Whether you think so or not, she's always been in your mind, in your heart. It's clear you haven't fully addressed this, honey. That charm isn't just a piece of plastic; it holds a deeper meaning. By getting that charm back, I'm sure you feel like you may be getting Amy back, but you won't. She's gone, honey."

Tears stream down my face as my mother wraps me tightly in her embrace. "She was practically family to us. It's not fair," I say through my sobs.

"I know it's not," she replies quietly. "But you have to keep going. Maybe visiting her gravesite will help. It will be hard, but it may provide the necessary closure."

The sight of Amy's name etched into a gravestone brings the heartbreaking finality of her death into achingly vivid focus. I think of the letter she wrote me, allowing her to say goodbye in her own words.

My heart is heavy with sorrow, and I know I must make this visit. It's my turn to bid my last farewell, no matter how challenging.

32

My dad calls out from the hallway as I grab my keys from the hook. "Where are you going?"

I pause, my hand on the doorknob. "The cemetery. To see Amy."

My dad steps closer, his brow furrowed. "Not at night, you're not."

My mom comes down the stairs. "Holly, I think we had a nice talk, but tomorrow is another day. It's cold and dark outside, and it's starting to snow. You've been through a lot today."

I can feel the emotions bubbling up inside of me. I *have* been through a lot, but all I want to do is talk to Amy one more time.

"What am I supposed to do? Do you want me to wallow in my room until it's warm, light, and there's no precipitation?"

"No one is suggesting you do that," my mom says gently. "I think you should eat something and rest."

"I will. Once I do this." I open the door, expecting more

resistance from my parents, when I hear voices. Levi and Owen are standing in my driveway.

My dad steps outside with me, ready to call the police. "What's going on here? Is everything okay?"

"I'll handle this, Dad."

He searches my face for any uncertainty, then places a hand on my shoulder and squeezes gently, as if to reassure me. With a slight tilt of his head, he silently conveys approval before turning away and heading inside. His gesture of faith fills me with confidence.

Once my dad is inside, I shove my hands in my coat pockets. I inhale deeply, the cold winter air rushing into my lungs, sharp and crisp. I can feel the chill on my tongue, and my breath comes out in a white cloud. There's an icy tingle in my nose. "What's going on here?"

They both give faint smiles, the tension between them still thick. A wave of dread waves over me; I don't want a repeat of last time, when Owen had been left lying on the ground, blood dripping from his nose.

Levi starts talking first. "When I left your house, Owen was sitting in the driveway in his car. We started talking."

"Have you decided who has the bigger penis?" Their egos are huge, Levi for punching Owen and Owen for holding the charm over my head.

"Come on, Holly. Don't be so crass," Owen responds, as though his opinion means anything to me.

"I'll be however I want to be, Owen. Why are you here? I don't have your money, and I never will."

"I don't want your money."

"Right," I laugh. "That's all you want."

Owen steps closer, his hand outstretched. Nestled within his calloused fingers is the charm. I keep my breath steady as I look into his eyes, searching for a sign that he wants something in return. But his expression is sincere, with no hint of a hidden agenda.

"I want you to have this back more than I want the money." I'm transfixed by the charm, unsure of what to do or say. "Here," he insists, pushing it into my hand. "What's wrong? Why won't you take it?"

"I'm waiting for the punchline," I reply, unable to believe that he's come to his senses.

"There's not one, Holly," Levi says. I almost forgot he was there. "Please, hear him out."

Levi's brows knit together as he clasps his hands. His expression is a mixture of urgency and desperation. He seemed to silently plead for me to take Owen's words seriously. That surprises me with their brief history, so for Levi for me to be recommending I hear Owen out must mean it's important.

"Fine." I grip the charm tightly in my hand. "What do you want to say?"

Owen waits for Levi to step out of earshot before talking. "I came after you when you left. I yelled for you, and you didn't respond. Either you didn't hear me, or you ignored me. Either way, I had to talk to you. When I came here, Levi was here. He was certainly the last person I wanted to see." He touches his nose, slightly bruised from when Levi hit him. "I asked him if he knew who you were talking about. He told me about Amy."

I force myself to swallow my tears as he says her name.

"Why didn't you tell me about her?"

I gaze down at the earth beneath me. "The pain of remembering her is sometimes too much to bear."

A deep sigh emanates from him. "I'm sorry. I acted like a jerk. I seriously thought this was just some dumb souvenir from a fair or something. I didn't realize it was so sentimental."

I look into his eyes, feeling a warmth spread through my chest, which catches me by surprise. For a moment, I see the old Owen, the one I had loved before the gambling had taken him over and destroyed our relationship.

"I know I'm a mess, Holly," he says, hanging his head. His eyes reflect the shame of his previous choices when he looks back at me. "I'm trying to do better. I really am. Sunny wasn't right for me, and I realized that after she left. I spiraled when I thought of my future because I didn't know what was there for me. You were the only good thing I had, and I messed that up."

I want to pull him into a warm embrace and assure him things will get better. "Owen, you have plenty to look forward to in life. I'm so happy you recognize that you need help. I want you to know I'm here for you as a friend."

His eyes widen. "Do you mean that?"

"Of course I do. Just don't be such a jerk." I cross my arms and stare at him.

He gazes at the snowflakes falling around us and scuffs his shoe through the thickening powder. "Okay, I deserve that. I don't know why I acted the way I did." His voice is heavy with guilt. "Fine, I do know why. Because I wanted someone to blame, I took it out on you and Levi."

The same way I'm blaming Levi for my lack of closure with Amy's death.

I force a smile and close my fist around the charm. "That's okay. I forgive you." I ignore the tightness in my throat, and a sense of ease washes over me. "Thank you, Owen. This means so much to me."

"I shouldn't have kept it from you. Please tell Levi no hard feelings about the other day. He was only trying to protect you. You've got a good guy there. Don't let him go." He cracks a small, soft smile.

"Thanks," I say. "I don't intend to." Taking a deep breath, I slowly turn and glance back at Levi. He's standing there, his hands tucked into his pockets. His eyes hold a warmth that wraps gently around my heart like a glove. Our bond is strong, and I know it will never fade.

❧ 33 ❧

After a long, difficult conversation full of tears, apologies, and promises, Levi and I come back from our argument stronger than ever. I wanted more than anything to go visit Amy, but in the end, Levi made the point that I'd waited this long, and waiting one evening wouldn't hurt. He suggested, like my parents, I wait until morning to go to the cemetery.

The next day, Levi pulls the car to a stop at the end of the picturesque walkway that winds through the cemetery. The sun is out, lighting up the eerily beautiful winter scene, casting a soft, comforting glow all around us. The groundskeeper must have been early to work this morning, leaving the path clear of the fresh snow that had covered the ground the night before.

"Are you sure you want to do this?" Levi asks, his voice gentle and full of understanding.

I swallow, feeling a lump form in my throat. "No," I whisper. "But I need to."

I gingerly open the door and step onto the icy gravel beneath me, which crunches softly beneath my feet. Levi grabs my hand, squeezing it reassuringly. "Come on, let's go."

We tread softly down the winding path, not a word passing between us. The cemetery exudes a tranquil atmosphere, and despite my apprehensions, I am strangely comforted by the thought of being reunited with Amy in this sacred place.

Levi guides me around the bend, his hand still tightly wrapped around mine. I'm forced to take a sharp intake of breath as we reach Amy's final resting place. Tears overflow from my eyes, and I cannot contain my sorrow. With a comforting embrace, Levi joins me in my grieving, and we spend a few moments together in this spot, united in our grief.

I kneel in the snow, unconcerned by the dampness seeping into my jeans. With a trembling hand, I trace the engraved name of my beloved friend, Amy Elizabeth Walsh. A silent prayer passes my lips, and I pause to steady my emotions. Taking a deep breath, I clasp the charm necklace in my palm, my thumb absently caressing its cold surface, as I prepare to offer a heartfelt tribute to Amy.

I choke back a sob, tears streaming down my cheeks as I whisper, "Hi Amy. It's me, Holly. I'm sorry I never found the courage to come to visit you. Every time I thought I could, I chickened out. Your brother, Levi, is here with me. He gave me your letter. I love you, Amy, and I'll cherish it forever." I wipe my eyes with my free hand. "I have something for you."

Levi places a comforting hand on my shoulder as I lean forward and delicately place the charm necklace on the ground next to her headstone.

"I want you to have this. It was our charm necklace. I thought I needed it, but I don't. I have the beautiful letter you wrote me, and I have Levi. Yes, we're together now, just like you wanted; we fit perfectly, and I think you always knew.

Maybe this necklace brought us together, so thank you for that."

Taking a few moments of silence, I remember the happy memories associated with the necklace. I can almost smell the popcorn and hear the delighted screams of the children on the Tilt-A-Whirl. That summer was scorching hot, with a drought, but it was one of the most enjoyable times for us. We were at the fair with her family and felt so grown up because they allowed us to wander off by ourselves. Her dad gave us each ten dollars to use for tickets and games.

I loved throwing darts at the balloons for a dollar and getting five tries. Although I wasn't particularly good at it, I still found success and won a small prize. After much deliberation, Amy and I chose a charm necklace as our reward. We took turns wearing it, and every time there was a school book fair, we'd buy a charm to add to it. Other girls our age had the 'Best Friends Forever' broken heart necklace to represent their friendship—we had this charm necklace that showed our bond.

Levi kneels next to me and drapes his strong arm around my shoulder. "Amy, it's Levi. I hope you're not tired of me yet. I know I've been here almost every day since moving back here. I miss you so much and think about you all the time. It's nice talking about you with Holly. You foresaw us together, didn't you?"

"She was always so smart," I say.

"Yes, she was. I remember when she won the state spelling bee. It was amazing to watch."

"And after she won the science fair three years in a row, her confidence was through the roof," I continued.

Levi smiles fondly and adds, "She was too brilliant for me. I certainly wouldn't have been able to compete with her."

We linger at the graveside, huddling together as the cold winter air seeps through our coats. Despite the cold, we remain there until our knees are nearly numb. Finally, when I feel I have said my goodbyes, I look at Levi, who has supported me throughout this journey.

"Thank you for being here with me," I say, taking his hand in mine. "It means so much."

"Of course," he answers, squeezing my hand. "I'm glad I could be here for you."

As we drive away, I can't help but wonder if Amy knows that I had come. I like to think that somehow she does. Regardless, I feel a sense of closure, knowing I was finally able to say goodbye.

Memories of my old job flood my mind as I walk through the sliding doors of the grocery store. I scan the aisles for familiar faces, but all that greets me is blank stares. I can almost hear a collective sigh of relief that I wasn't here to demand overtime or whip them into a frenzy of increased efficiency. Christmas Eve is never anyone's favorite day to work.

I begin to walk down the aisles and put items into my cart. The first aisle has most of the ingredients I need for the dinner I'm preparing for my parents, Vivienne, Cal, and Levi. As I pick up the different items, the thought of being able to provide a meal for them makes my heart swell; it feels like it is my way of saying thank you for always being there for me.

Passing by the door leading to my old office, where Crystal fired me, I take a deep breath and keep going, pushing away any negative thoughts as best as I can. Just a few more items left to get, and I can be out of here.

I round the corner, my cart leading the way, and almost crash into someone. Before I see the face, the voice tells me all I need to know—Crystal.

What does the universe have against me?

"Holly!" she exclaims, throwing her hands up in surprise. She's wearing her signature bright red lipstick and an oversized blush-colored sweater. The strong smell of her perfume is so overwhelming that I can taste it in the air, a bitter reminder of her presence.

I give Crystal a tight-lipped smile as I grip the card handle, unsure how to respond to her greeting. Our last conversation was when she fired me. She seems sincere, though, as she says, "It's wonderful to see you."

Hesitantly, I ask, "It is?"

She smiles and nods, her eyes brightening as she assures me, "Yes. You've been on my mind quite a bit lately."

"Why is that, Ms. Silver?"

She places her hand on the end of my cart as if to hold me in place in case I try to run. She wants my full, undivided attention.

"This isn't easy for me to say. I don't like admitting I'm wrong. I know I didn't do the right thing in this case."

"What are you talking about?"

"I accused you of bringing drugs into the store without investigating. I now know Scottie had the drugs, and I regret letting you go for something you weren't responsible for. I'm truly sorry for the pain and disappointment I caused you. I hope you can find it in your heart to forgive me."

The impulse to say, "I told you so," is strong, but I bite my lip and hold back the words. This isn't the time to gloat. "Thank you," I say, and I mean it. "That means a lot, and I appreciate it."

Crystal averts her eyes for a second and then takes a deep breath. She bites her lip, leaving a trace of lipstick on her teeth. "I know it's a long shot, but do you think there's any chance you'd take your old job back?"

I can feel a chuckle bubbling up from the pit of my stomach, but I manage to contain it. Instead, I take a deep breath and try to keep my composure, hoping that my face isn't betraying my inner laughter.

"Thank you for the apology. I've found something else, though."

"Really?" she asks with an uncomfortable abundance of shock. "You didn't take a job at one of those big corporate stores, did you?"

"No. I'm not in retail anymore. I started a job as a graphic designer for a firm on Penrose Street."

Her eyes widen, and she brings her hand to her mouth. "Oh, Penrose Street. Look at you." She walks around me, her gaze taking in my winter jacket, jeans, and knit hat. The look of surprise on her face makes it clear she expected something fancier for someone working on Penrose Street. Sure, I dress up for work, but I'm not *at* work. "How do you like it?"

"I haven't been there long, but it's a good fit so far."

"I see," she murmurs, tapping her index finger against her lips. She fixes a steady gaze on me, and I can tell she's trying to think of a way to convince me to return.

I shake my head before she can say anything. Firing me has been a blessing; I have moved on with my life. "I do think you should consider Nora for management."

"Nora?" she asks, as if she has no idea who she is, but I know she does.

"Yes, Nora. She's probably the best employee here. She's always on time, works well with everyone, and her critical thinking skills are fabulous. I considered her my second-hand. I could always count on her."

Crystal nods. "I'll think about it. I don't want to be on the sales floor another day." A hint of desperation tinges in her voice.

"Wait. You're the manager right now?"

She shrugs. "Someone has to be, and I haven't had time to

hire or train someone else. Once I found out what Scottie did, I let him go immediately."

"Trust me. Nora is the one you need." I don't owe anything to her. I'm only making the suggestion to help Nora, not Crystal. "If you'll excuse me, I must finish shopping so I can get home and start making dinner."

"Oh!" Crystal exclaims, seeming offended I'm ending the conversation, not her. "Please, don't let me keep you from your... pasta," she says, glancing at my grocery cart. She looks at me as though I'm committing a crime by making pasta on Christmas Eve.

"Sure," I reply, and as soon as she steps out of the way, I hurry down the aisle, never once looking back, sure I'm on the path to a brighter future.

❧ 35 ❧

On Christmas morning, I slowly stir in Levi's embrace, feeling the warmth of his body radiating onto mine. I feel a sense of comfort and security wrapped up in his strong arms, and I'm thankful for my bond with him. Although leaving my parent's house for the night was a bit strange, I can't deny the joy I have in being with Levi, especially on such a special day. After all, I'm almost forty and make my own decisions.

The morning sunlight spills through the windows, casting a golden hue against the Christmas tree in the corner of his living room. There aren't any presents underneath this year, seeing as our relationship is so new, but I expect it to be overflowing next year.

Wow. I'm already thinking about my *next* Christmas with Levi.

I want to make a special breakfast for us, so I prepare fluffy scrambled eggs, toast, and bacon. The aroma of coffee wafts from the brewer, and I'm warm before I even take a sip. The prospect of having a cozy morning with my partner is incredibly appealing, and I'm excited to start the day. I'm so thankful for the love and support Levi has given me, and I'm looking forward to spending the rest of the day together.

When I finish making breakfast, I call Levi into the kitchen. He stumbles into the room, his hair a tangled mess. He still is as handsome as ever, his white shirt accentuating his broad shoulders and strong arms, and his gray sweatpants hanging just right on his hips.

What is it about gray sweatpants that make women feral?

"Merry Christmas, darling," he says, pressing his full lips to my shoulder and neck. I moan a little and tilt my head to give him better access. His stubble scratches against my skin, making me tingle with the familiar feeling of love. I didn't think it was possible for me ever to be this happy.

"Merry Christmas," I say back. "I got you something," I tell him as I wipe my hands on the towel.

"You didn't have to get me anything."

"I know. It's small." I pull the framed picture out of my oversized purse. "In fact, I didn't even wrap it."

He takes the frame from me, and his eyes light up when he looks at it. "This is us at the ice castles."

I move closer and run my hand over his back. "Our first real date, and when I knew you were someone special."

He turns and presses his lips against mine. His lips are soft and warm, melting into mine as easily as butter. He presses them with gentle pressure, allowing them to linger for a moment before pulling away. "I have something for you, too," he says.

Levi reaches into the pocket of his sweats and pulls out a holiday-wrapped rectangular box. The image on the paper is a collage of *The Simpsons* characters, all wearing Santa hats. I feel as if I've stepped back in time; the 1990s beckoning me to return.

But I don't want to go back. I'm happy where I am now.

I run my fingernail on the crease of the paper, taking care

to open it. A black box reveals itself. I take the lid off and see a beautiful shining silver bracelet.

"What's this?" I ask as I slowly take it out of the box.

"It's a charm bracelet. And I plan to give you a new charm to add to it every year. And this," he says, reaching into his pocket and pulling out a small heart-shaped charm outlined in diamonds, "is to get it started." He clips it on.

"This is gorgeous, Levi." I hold my arm before me and watch the charm dangle.

"I know how much the necklace you had meant to you. This isn't meant to be a replacement. It represents our love because I love you."

My heart swells with joy, and a solitary tear rolls down my cheek as he runs the back of his hand across it. "You do?"

"I always have," he replies. "I've waited for this day to come."

"I love you, too." After all this time, my life is coming together.

Levi leans forward and kisses me, and I finally feel I have everything I ever wanted.

I NESTLE INTO LEVI'S STRONG ARMS AS WE SIT ON THE couch with a soft, cozy blanket draped over our legs. He pulls me closer and nuzzles his nose against my cheek. "This is the most perfect Christmas morning I've ever had." His lips trace my jawline, and I close my eyes, savoring the warmth of his touch.

"I'm right there with you," I tell him, my heart full. Our day will soon become a flurry of activity as we visit his dad and then spend the evening with my parents, Viv, and Cal. But I don't mind the hustle and bustle; there's no feeling quite like being surrounded by the people you love.

Levi gives a heavy sigh, his eyes fixed on the view outside the window. "I really miss her," he says softly.

I shift closer and drape my arm around his shoulders, knowing he means Amy. "I do, too," I murmur.

"She would've loved this. If she were here, she'd be belting out that darn *Alvin and the Chipmunks* Christmas song because she knew I couldn't stand it." He chuckles fondly. "I'd do anything to have her bother me with it just one more time."

His words spark an idea, and I pull away slightly, reaching for my phone. "What are you up to?" he asks.

I smile and reply, "Just wait and see." I pull up my music app and search for the song. Once I find it, I press play, and the cheerful tune fills the room.

He cringes at the sound, but the sparkle in his eyes gives away his delight. He leaps off the couch and pulls me close, and we dance, singing the words together until our laughter echoes through the room.

He turns to me, his gaze brimming with affection. "Thank you. You know exactly how to make me smile." Without another word, he leans in, and our lips meet in a passionate kiss, like a blazing fire on a winter's night.

Though winter was never my favorite, Levi changed that. His love for me is like a storybook coming to life. He's shown me that I'm worthy of a love that will last forever, and I'm so thankful that I get to experience it with him. Our charming winter has been a beautiful journey, and I wouldn't want to share it with anyone else.

❧ 36 ❧

THE FOLLOWING SUMMER

My apartment is the perfect little oasis. I'm lucky to have found a place with a bit of privacy and a landlord that doesn't mind minor changes, such as wall color. With Viv's expert help, I painted the walls with inviting colors and hung the most beautiful decor. We also spruced up the patio with a table, chairs, and a lounger for me to enjoy my two trees and the hammock slung between them.

The place is small, but it has everything I need; a bedroom, bathroom, eat-in kitchen, and living room. Best of all, it's mine. I worked hard over the past six months at Kent Illuminations and saved enough to afford my own apartment and pay off some of my debt.

Although I haven't paid off every last cent, I'm comfortable now. I'm also relieved to find out that Owen has joined Gamblers Anonymous and is now walking a path of recovery. I'm happy for him.

I cross my arms and lean against the patio doorway, watching everyone laughing. All the people I love are here;

Levi, my parents, Viv, Cal, Sadie, Joe, their daughter Rose, Dani, and even Dani's daughter, Neveah. I can't believe how perfect life is right now.

"You did an amazing job." Levi sets the ketchup and mustard on the table before kissing me on the cheek.

"Thank you." I squeeze him tightly when he pulls me into a hug. "I have Viv to thank for a lot of it. And you, of course, for being the grill master today."

Levi picks up the spatula and twirls it. "Hot dogs and burgers? I can handle that." He smooches the top of my head. "And with you by my side, I can handle anything."

I gaze at the charm bracelet on my wrist. I've added one more charm since Levi gave it to me—a tree, its branches representing all the people in my life, both present and past, a beautiful tapestry of my life.

As I observe the love around me, I can't believe how lucky I am. No matter what the future brings, Amy will always be with me. And this life I'm starting with Levi fits perfectly, like it was supposed to be like this from the beginning.

Maybe it was.

THANK YOU FOR READING!

Please consider leaving a review on your favorite book retailer's website! Sign up for Tracy's newsletter at www.tracykrimmer.com/newsletter to stay up to date with new releases, including when Dani's story is ready!

ACKNOWLEDGMENTS

This book has been a long time time coming. I finished writing the first draft in November 2021. Two charity projects came along and this book was put on the back burner as I participated in those.

One of those limited anthologies, Dissent, raised money for reproductive rights and also hit the USA Today Bestseller list.

Hitting a list has always been a dream of mine.

As of this book's publication date, the list is no longer. That won't take away the excitement and pride of reaching that goal with such an amazing group of people.

I wish Lin had been alive to see this.

The person I dedicated this book to, Lin, was a former teacher of mine. She taught me creative writing in high school (many moons ago!). Over the past few years, we connected online sharing many of the same interests and values. While she did not see the anthology hit the USA Today Bestseller list, she did read the story I had in there, called "Pushing Her Buttons." After she read it, she wrote on my social media page, *"I just read your story in Dissent. It was a wonderful story with solid prose and a good sense of what a good story needs to flow. It's so cool seeing one of my writing students writing so well."*

I will always remember her and her amazing words. She was honest and outspoken, and she loved posting about her beloved grandchildren and her dogs. The world has suffered an incredible loss with her passing, but the world is also so much better with her having been in it.

I am so grateful to everyone who has supported me in my writing career and this book. To my husband, thank you for everything you do to make this dream possible. To my kids, I'm sorry I'm "cringe," but I promise you will be too one day!

And thank you, dear readers, for putting your trust in me and my words, and most of all, for taking a chance on me.

ABOUT THE AUTHOR

Tracy Krimmer loves coffee, books, naps, and the 80s and 90s. On a typical day you'll find her writing at one of her favorite spots-on the couch, at the kitchen table, or at her favorite hometown coffee shop.

Make sure to subscribe to her fabulous weekly newsletter at www.tracykrimmer.com/newsletter.

ALSO BY TRACY KRIMMER

Novels

Novellas